# HOMETOWN HOME RUN

ANNIE RAINS

ISBN-13: 978-1-335-52914-5

Hometown Home Run



For questions and comments about the quality of this book, please contact us at CustomerService@Harlequin.com.



Love Inspired
22 Adelaide St. West, 41st Floor
Toronto, Ontario M5H 4E3, Canada
www.LoveInspired.com

HarperCollins Publishers
Macken House, 39/40 Mayor Street Upper,
Dublin 1, D01 C9W8, Ireland
www.HarperCollins.com

**Printed in Lithuania**

1 2 3 4 5 6 7 8 9 10 LIT 28 27 26 25

## “There’s a spot on this team for anyone who wants it…

“Your son can use a lightweight bat and a tee for hitting. And I can assign a peer runner for the bases.” Daniel’s eyes lit up as he proposed the accommodations he’d come up with, reminding Adaline of the boy who used to spend hours telling her about baseball strategies. “The Little League rules allow for disability accommodations. We just need to be creative,” he said with a shrug. “I’m not about to let Will crash on my watch.”

“Wow,” Adaline said quietly. “It sounds like you’ve thought this out.” Looking at him now, explaining adaptive baseball techniques with such enthusiasm, Adaline felt her carefully constructed walls begin to waver. This wasn’t the same Daniel she’d convinced herself that she never wanted to see again.

The man standing before her was someone who’d clearly done his research in a matter of hours since seeing them at the grocery store, just to make sure Will felt included.

But trusting Daniel with her son scared her far more than trusting him with her own heart.

**Annie Rains** is a contemporary author of over twenty books centered around small towns and family. Annie lives in her own small town in North Carolina with her husband and three children. Raised in a Christian home, Annie weaves elements of love, faith and family into her books, reflecting flawed characters in need of a personal transformation—the kind only God can provide. To learn more about Annie, visit www.annierains.com.

**Books by Annie Rains**

**Love Inspired**

*Healing His Widowed Heart* (as Annie Hemby)
*Hometown Home Run*

Visit the Author Profile page at LoveInspired.com.

But as for you, ye thought evil against me;
but God meant it unto good, to bring to pass,
as it is this day, to save much people alive.
—*Genesis* 50:20

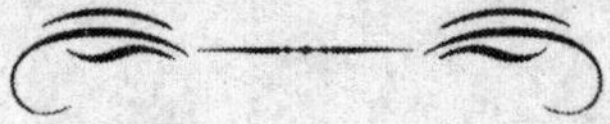

To the real-life prodigal pastor,
whose tests became a testament to God's grace.

# *Chapter One*

Adaline Harper watched in awe as her eight-year-old son worked through his morning stretches with more persistence than most adults she knew.

"Remember to breathe through it, sweetie," she encouraged, noticing the way his cheeks flushed as he held his breath. She stepped farther into Will's room and sat on the side of his Lightning McQueen–themed bed. Will liked McQueen because he was fast, whereas Will's cerebral palsy diagnosis caused him to be slower than most, or all, of his peers. Will's legs trembled with the effort of the stretches that his physical therapist had taught him, his muscles fighting against his constant spasticity.

"Here, let me help." Adaline gently placed a hand on his lower back, guiding him into the stretch. "Look how much farther you're getting in these stretches."

Will paused to give her a smile, revealing a recent missing tooth. "I can reach the freckle above my knee when I stretch now. Last week I could only touch the scar from when I fell in PE last year."

Adaline laughed, releasing her hand from his back and helping him move from the floor to his walker. "See? Hard work pays off. From a scar to a freckle in one week. Who knows what you'll be able to do next month."

"I know what I'll be able to do," he said. "*If* you say yes."

Something about the flash of desperation in his eyes worried her. Will liked to ask permission to participate in things that he physically couldn't, giving her the impossible job of saying yes and watching him fail or telling him no and being the bad guy.

"Carson's joining the Prairie Dogs Little League team." Will white-knuckled the handles of his walker as he looked up at her with those bright hazel eyes, so much like his father's.

"Baseball?" Adaline asked, her stomach tightening. She knew what was coming next.

"Mom, I want to play too."

Adaline busied herself with adjusting his shirt to buy time before responding. "Sweetheart, baseball might be a little… challenging." She didn't like discouraging him from anything, but it was his reality. Cerebral palsy was a physical disability with limitations that couldn't be ignored.

"Because I'm different?" Will's tone of voice was matter-of-fact. "Because my body doesn't always do what I want it to?"

"That's right. And baseball involves running." Whereas standing was sometimes difficult for Will. "Your body is expected to respond quickly. Those balls fly through the air and—"

"But Mom," he interrupted, his chin lifting stubbornly. His words came out slightly slower now, his heightened emotions affecting his speech. "You always tell me my name is special because God gave us free will. You say we can do anything we put our minds and hearts to."

Adaline swallowed hard. Trust her son to use her own words against her. *Please help me, God,* she prayed silently as she assisted Will in maneuvering toward the bathroom. The walker caught briefly on the bathroom rug but Will managed to free himself just like he'd learned in his therapy sessions.

"We can discuss this more later," she said. "Right now, we need to focus on getting ready for school."

Will needed to get to third grade and she had to head to her own classroom, where she worked as a reading specialist at Prairie Elementary.

"I know I can do it, Mom," Will pressed. He looked at her through their reflection in the mirror, standing straighter. "I believe in myself."

How could she argue that? "I know Coach Milo's wife from church," she said with a slight nod, preparing his toothbrush. "Maybe we could see if there's a way for you to help out with the team. Perhaps you can keep score. Or cheer them on."

"You want me to be a cheerleader?" Will's face fell slightly. "Mom, I want to play ball." He grabbed the toothbrush from her hand and frowned as a drop of toothpaste hit his shirt. His eyes immediately welled up. "Now I have to change clothes!" His voice cracked and his expression crumpled as he fought back tears. It wasn't because of the spot of toothpaste. She knew that. He was smart enough to sense when her "maybe" meant "no."

"Hey." Adaline grabbed a washcloth. "It's just a tiny spot. We can dab it right out." She worked quickly to clean the spot and then met his teary gaze. "Let me think about it, okay? No promises."

"Do you promise to think about it?" he asked. "Please."

Her eyes stung too. Even if he didn't have physical limitations, getting him to and from games would be another responsibility in her already packed schedule. Being a single working mother of a child with special needs was like trying to solve a puzzle where the pieces kept changing shape. She loved Will though. He was her greatest blessing and she wanted the very best for him. Was that baseball though?

"I promise."

Once they were both dressed and ready for school, Adaline helped Will out the door and down the steps with his book bag and walker in tow. The North Carolina air was cool, the faint smell of azaleas in bloom carrying on the slight breeze this morning. She wished she had time to stop and smell the roses, or azaleas in this scenario, but school mornings were busy. Every day as a single mother was.

After helping Will get buckled in the back of her car and loading his walker, Adaline slid behind the steering wheel and turned the key in the ignition, her heart dropping when the engine didn't turn over. She tried again, her gaze flicking to meet Will's in the back seat.

"Please, help us, God," Will prayed out loud. Then he cheered when she turned the key a third time and the engine purred to life. "See, Mom. God listens when I pray. I also prayed that you would let me play ball."

She smiled at him in the rearview. Sweet, stubborn and full of faith—that was her son. "Let's go to school."

A few minutes later, they pulled into the school's parking lot. Adaline retrieved Will's walker from the trunk and helped Will out of the car. Once he was standing, she assisted him in putting on his book bag. "Are you sure you don't want me to carry that for you?"

Will gave her a look that she could read as well as any book on her shelf. Mr. Independent himself could carry his own bag. Because Adaline also worked in the school, she got a few perks like dropping Will off early so that he could be his "teacher's helper."

"Will!" Miss Woodrich said with a bright smile. "I've been waiting on you." She pointed at a stack of papers on her horseshoe-shaped table. "All of those deserve stickers. Can you put one at the top of each for me?"

Will's excitement was palpable. And the extra fine-motor-skill work would make Will's occupational therapist happy too.

"Thank you," Adaline mouthed with a wave before hurrying toward her own class to prepare for the day. Her thoughts returned to the conversation about baseball as she walked, her smile slowly falling as she realized this was one of those requests she couldn't grant.

"Either you're having the same kind of Monday that I am, or you heard the news," Mrs. Lindsay, one of the other teachers, said.

"Hmm?" Adaline blinked the teacher into focus. "What news?"

Mrs. Lindsay cupped a hand to her mouth as she took a step closer. "Daniel Matthews is back in town."

The name sent an unwelcome flutter through Adaline's chest. She and Daniel had been high school sweethearts and once upon a time she'd thought they would marry, have kids and live happily ever after. That, along with her dream of being an author, had faded fast with adulthood.

"Daniel comes to town several times a year," Adaline said. "He was just here at Christmas." And everyone knew that Pastor Matthews was sick with pneumonia right now. Surely Daniel was here to see his father. Hopefully for just a one- or two-day well-check and then he'd go back to Atlanta, like he always did. Adaline started to continue toward her classroom, but Mrs. Lindsay's next words stopped her in her tracks.

"I think this stay is going to be more than a brief visit. My sources tell me Daniel is *back* back."

Adaline slowly turned and raised a questioning eyebrow. Small-town sources were nothing if not unreliable.

Mrs. Lindsay attended the same church as Adaline and they worked together. Adaline was in the same news grapevine, and she hadn't heard anything about Daniel moving home for good.

"Lauralyn told me Daniel has moved back to help out with the family farm."

"I thought Pastor Matthews was on the mend," Adaline said.

"Double pneumonia at his age?" Mrs. Lindsay shook her head. "Tending horses and chickens ain't for the faint. Even when he's well, he'll need to build back his strength and endurance."

That made sense. Suddenly the hallway seemed to tilt and her vision dimmed. Avoiding Daniel during his brief visits was one thing but Prairie was the kind of small town where everyone's paths crossed on a near daily basis. Prairie only had one grocery store, a post office and three restaurants on Main Street. If Daniel was truly back for any length of time...

Adaline gripped her insulated coffee mug tighter. In the past ten years, she'd managed to turn the other direction and walk away every single time they'd had a near run-in. She didn't want to face him because, even though years had passed, she wasn't sure what her reaction would be. She'd either want to scream or, worse, she'd rush into his arms to hug him.

"Well, that's nice for Pastor and Mrs. Matthews," she said, speaking of the pastor's family, whom she'd once thought would be her own family someday. "Have a nice day, Mrs. Lindsay."

Once Adaline was alone in her classroom, she braced herself on the back of a student's chair, closed her eyes and sent up a silent SOS. *God, if this is true, please help me.* She was going to need assistance hiding her feelings, which were a mix of bitter and sweet. Because there was something else she was hiding from Daniel.

*For there is nothing covered, that shall not be revealed; neither hid, that shall not be known.*

The scripture came to her mind the way it often did this past year since becoming baptized. Adaline's best friend, Beth, whose own son was Will's best friend, had invited Will to vacation Bible school three summers ago and Will had rarely missed a Sunday since. Adaline's stubbornness had kept her from going with him, though, until last year. Adaline had worried that her attending the church pastored by her ex's father would be awkward. When she'd finally gone, however, at Will's insistence, everything in her life changed.

Building a relationship with God had filled a void in her life. Where her earthly father had failed her, her heavenly one had lifted her up, molding her into a new person. A better mother for Will. And the closer she'd drawn to God over the past year, the more she felt the pressing need in her heart to come clean with her past, and with Daniel.

Daniel Matthews wiped sweat from his brow as he finished mucking out the last stall. He'd loathed the chore most when he was growing up with a father who not only pastored a church but also kept horses.

Star, his father's oldest mare, nickered softly, likely laughing at Daniel. He wasn't a boy trying to earn extra cash anymore. Instead, Daniel was nearly thirty years old and shoveling manure. He recalled the young man he'd been when he left Prairie eight years ago. Young and foolish.

His last failed business venture in Atlanta was a start-up consulting firm that had hemorrhaged money for six straight months. It still haunted him. Not only had he lost his own savings but he'd also lost the small investment that his parents had made in an effort to support him. Regardless of what he did, they'd always had his back. The food truck fiasco in

Nashville. A subscription box service for pet owners that never made it past the planning stage. The ideas had popped up like dandelions and he'd gone for them, more desperate with each failed endeavor.

For months now, he'd felt God tugging him home, but pride had kept him anchored in Atlanta, determined to prove himself. Even after his consulting firm folded, he'd kept sending out résumés and making cold calls. He didn't want to be like the prodigal son of the Bible, but if his mom hadn't called him last week, asking him to consider coming home to help during his father's illness, Daniel would have called her. He was broke and his spirit was broken.

Guilt furled in Daniel's stomach. When his mom had called, he'd let her believe she was asking a huge favor. The truth was, being invited back home to have a roof over his head and nutritious meals was the answer to his prayers. He just wished the reason wasn't that his dad was sick.

Daniel finished giving Star her evening feed and checked on the other two horses before heading toward the brick ranch-style home of his childhood. Yesterday, he'd mowed some of his family's twenty-five acres. There was still more to mow along with weed eating and a dozen other things. It was no wonder his dad couldn't do it while he was recovering from double pneumonia. Daniel was amazed his father could do it before his illness.

Daniel picked up his pace when the house came into view.

His mother turned from the stove as he walked in. "Daniel! Oh, good. Honey, could you run to the grocery store down the road for some butter? I need it for dinner."

Right now, all he wanted was a cold glass of water and a steaming-hot shower, but he kissed her cheek and grabbed his keys from the counter. "Sure, Mom. Is Dad okay?"

"I think the prayers and antibiotics are working." She patted his arm. "He asked about you this morning. He wanted to know if you'd taken Star out for her exercise yet."

Daniel's throat tightened. Obviously, he wasn't cut out to be a businessman nor was he made for farming. "I took her out this morning."

His mother's hand lifted to pat his cheek gently. "We are so grateful to have your help, son." Lowering her hand, she made a shooing motion. "Now go on. If I don't get butter, you and your father won't eat."

"Can't have that. I'm starving."

Daniel opted to drive his father's old pickup as he went into town, trying to blend in as much as possible. He didn't want to answer a bunch of questions right now, like how long was he staying and how was his career going. The answers would only yield more questions that he didn't have answers for. All he knew was that for now, he was tending his dad's farm and coaching the Prairie Dogs Little League team for his childhood friend Milo, who needed to be home with his wife and newborn baby. At least the coaching job would bring in a small paycheck, but he would have stepped up to coach for free. At last night's introduction, the kids had been enthusiastic and eager to learn. Getting back on the field was going to be fun, which was something Daniel hadn't had in a while. When your finances and career goals were spiraling, fun was the furthest thing from one's mind.

"God, please give me some guidance," he prayed out loud. His father was sick, but double pneumonia would heal. His dad would get back on his feet and Milo would return to coaching after his paternity leave. Daniel didn't want to go back to his old life though. He needed a compass, he thought, pulling into the grocery store parking lot.

The bell above Morgan's Grocery chimed as Daniel entered, and he immediately spotted Mrs. Henderson from his father's congregation as she examined tomatoes. He thought about ducking into aisle two, but not before she looked up and smiled.

"Daniel Matthews, is that you? Oh, dear, how is your father doing? We've all been so worried."

Relief about the topic of conversation poured over him, followed quickly by shame. Here he was, worried about himself when his father was the one suffering. "He's improving, Mrs. Henderson. Thank you for asking. Your prayers are appreciated."

She reached out and squeezed his arm. "We'll keep them coming."

Daniel chatted a few minutes more and then continued down the outer aisle toward the dairy case. He'd almost made it to the register with the butter his mom wanted when he felt a tap on his lower arm. Looking down, he found himself face-to-face with a young boy white-knuckling the handles of a walker.

"You're the new coach for the Prairie Dogs," the boy said, his hazel eyes bright with recognition.

Daniel remembered seeing the kid on the bleachers last night during team introductions. He'd been sitting with the parent of one of the team members and Daniel had assumed the boy was a sibling. "Yes, I am. I'm Coach Daniel."

The boy's face broke into a grin and he stuck out his hand with surprising determination. "Hello, Coach Daniel. My name is Will and I want to be a Prairie Dog."

Daniel was speechless for a moment, leaving the kid's hand extended. He wasn't sure if he'd misunderstood.

Will's arm wavered in the air, shaking slightly against gravity as he waited, his face strained with determination.

Not wanting to leave him hanging, Daniel carefully took Will's hand. "Wow. That's quite a grip you've got there."

Daniel wasn't exaggerating. For such a small kid with obvious disabilities, his grasp was strong.

"Get your hands off my son!" a woman's voice demanded, slicing through the air like a knife.

Daniel's hand dropped back to his side and his head snapped up. There, standing at the end of the aisle with fire in her eyes, was his first love, the girl he'd pushed away after a series of other life-changing mistakes in his youth.

"Adaline."

"Mommm," Will protested, his voice carrying a hint of embarrassment. "This is Coach Daniel, the new baseball coach. I was introducing myself."

Adaline's expression shifted from anger to confusion to something else entirely. He'd seen her more than a dozen times since they were eighteen, but usually it was just the back of her, walking briskly away to presumably avoid him. Now he had an up-close view of her face, framed by light brown hair, shorter than it used to be. She still had that stubborn chin, he noticed, but the spark in her eyes that used to be so bright was dimmer, barely visible above the dark circles that underscored them.

"Daniel," she said, his name coming out like a sigh.

"I didn't..." Daniel's heart was suddenly racing. "I didn't know this was your son." He'd heard, of course, that she had a son, but he'd purposely never asked or let his curiosity get the better of him. Thinking of Adaline apart from him was painful even though he was the one who'd ended things.

Will looked between them. "Mom, you know Coach Daniel?"

She cleared her throat. "Yes, I do. We went to school together," she answered, moving closer to Will. "A long time ago."

She was a year younger than Daniel and she'd only started

Prairie High during Daniel's senior year. He'd barely known her until late that winter.

"Mom, you remember how I told you that I really want to play baseball? I've been praying all day and look. Coach Daniel is here!" Will said, excitedly. "That means God heard me and He's answering my prayer, right?"

Daniel watched the conflicting emotions sweep across Adaline's face.

"We'll talk about it at home, sweetie." Her voice softened when she spoke to Will. "Right now though, we need to get going or we'll be late for your physical therapy appointment." She looked at Daniel, her cheeks darkening. "It was nice to see you," she said quietly.

Daniel wondered if she meant it. "You too," he said, with all sincerity. He watched them go, the butter forgotten in his hands, feeling like maybe God had heard his prayers as well. He had asked God to show him where he needed to be and what he needed to be doing. Somehow, he thought Adaline and her son were the answer, even though that made no sense in his own mind. God's ways were higher though. He hadn't realized that in high school, but he understood it now. He didn't need to know the why; he just needed to say okay when God came calling.

# *Chapter Two*

Adaline's hands shook as she dialed her friend Beth's number from the parking lot of Will's physical therapy clinic, where he came once a week to work on exercises and stretching.

"You'll never guess who I just ran into," she said as soon as Beth answered.

"Hmm. Let me guess. Our new baseball coach?" Beth's voice held a hint of amusement. "I was wondering when you'd call."

Adaline's grip tightened on her steering wheel. "You knew Daniel Matthews was coaching the Prairie Dogs?"

"Of course I did." Beth sighed into the phone's receiver. "Coach Milo is taking some paternity leave, and Daniel just moved back to help Pastor Matthews while he's recovering. It just made sense."

"It made sense to put my ex in charge of coaching the baseball team that my son is currently obsessed with?" Adaline mentally reminded herself to take deep breaths because she was letting this affect her way too much.

Beth's voice softened. "I know it's not easy facing the man who broke your heart."

Adaline flinched. "Ancient history."

"Good. Then seeing Daniel shouldn't be a problem. It's not like you haven't seen him in all these years."

Adaline had seen Daniel plenty of times but she'd always

turned the other direction, avoiding anything more than a wave or brief pleasantry. After their breakup, Adaline had married Christopher within six months, hiding in a marriage and then motherhood. She'd cut off the part of her that had loved Daniel. She never allowed herself to even think about him, which was easier said than done.

"Will wants to play," she told Beth.

"Carson told me." Carson, Beth's son, was the same age as Will. "And I think it's great."

Adaline couldn't believe what she was hearing. "You think it's great that my son with cerebral palsy wants to play baseball?"

"You're the one who's always saying we shouldn't put limits on what he can do, right?"

Adaline shook her head. "He physically can't, Beth. He's been in PT for years just to walk a safe distance on his own. Baseball involves running. Quick movements. Holding a heavy bat and swinging it. I mean, when he first asked to play, I considered checking with Milo about a bench position for Will to do, just to feel included. But now, knowing Daniel is coaching…"

"Adaline, are you really going to let your history with Daniel hold Will back?"

The question hung in the air, heavy with truth. Adaline had spent eight years encouraging Will to push boundaries and try new things. She never wanted him to let his disability define him.

But this wasn't just about Will's limitations. It was about the man who'd promised her forever under the Friday-night lights of Prairie High's football field. The one who'd shared dreams about a little white house with a wraparound porch where they'd raise their family. This was about the guy who'd promised he'd never break Adaline's heart, right before doing exactly that.

She'd been foolishly sure that Daniel was "the one" back then. She knew he'd made drastic life changes before he'd started hanging out with her, but she hadn't really considered what that meant for him. He'd grown up in a Christian home and had planned to attend seminary prior to their relationship, but then he'd switched gears. Young adults did that all the time. Somehow, she naively thought he wouldn't change his mind about her though.

After leaving for college, Daniel went from texting hourly to brief one-word responses every twenty-four hours. He didn't come home that first weekend like he'd promised. Or the next one. When he had finally ended things just three weeks after leaving Prairie, he'd said it was because he needed to focus on making something of himself. As if loving her was holding him back.

"Adaline?" Beth asked, pulling her out of her memories.

"I don't like it when you're right," Adaline muttered into the phone, returning to the present moment.

"Which is often," Beth teased. Then her voice softened. "Maybe it's time to let go of the past. We're not those kids anymore, you know."

No, they weren't. That naive girl who'd believed in forever had been replaced by a mother who understood that some promises couldn't be kept, no matter how sincerely they were made. And now that same man who'd shattered her trust wanted to coach her beautiful, determined, vulnerable son who wore his heart on his sleeve just like she used to before the world had callused it.

"See you at practice tomorrow night?" Beth asked.

"Sure." Adaline really didn't have much choice. As a single parent, she was tasked with most everything in her son's life. She wasn't going to get out of Little League practice and games, and she wouldn't want to miss watching Will participate anyway. Beth was right about them being adults now, and as an adult, Adaline knew how to stand up for herself these days—and for her son. If Daniel broke Will's heart the way he had hers, he'd be sorry.

The following evening, Adaline's heart pounded as she pushed Will's long-distance wheelchair across the baseball field. He was practically vibrating with excitement as they approached the dugout where Daniel stood checking the equipment.

"Hello there," he said, looking up as they approached.

"Hi, Coach!" Will said enthusiastically, reaching down to take control of his chair himself.

Adaline pulled her hands from the handles and forced herself to meet Daniel's eyes. "Hi. Can we, um, talk?"

"Of course." Daniel stepped away from the dugout. Wearing a Prairie Dogs coach shirt and baseball cap, he looked so much like his eighteen-year-old self that it made her chest ache. Once upon a time, the man in front of her could do no wrong in her eyes. She'd never met anyone like him before and she'd fallen for him so fast and so completely.

"What's going on?" he asked.

Adaline glanced over at Will, who was watching them intently. "Will, sweetheart, can you take my bag to the bleachers while Coach Daniel and I discuss a few things?" Will's wheelchair had an electric function that allowed him to operate it with his right hand.

She saw the hesitation in his eyes, pleading with her not to change her mind about letting him play. "Sure, Mom," he said obediently.

"Thank you." Adaline watched as Will maneuvered across

the field. When he was out of earshot, she turned to Daniel. "My son would like to be part of the team. I was thinking that maybe he could help take score. Or fill water bottles."

Daniel folded his arms over his chest as he listened to her list off a few more ideas that she'd spent all last night coming up with. Finally, he shook his head. "We don't have spots like that on this team, Addie."

Her body tensed under his nickname for her. He was the only one who'd ever called her that. "I see." Heat rose from her chest. Here she was, intent on leaving the past behind them for the sake of her son, but apparently, Daniel hadn't matured since high school. "Kids with special needs may not be able to do everything their peers can, but they can still participate. Will uses a walker and sometimes even a wheelchair but—"

"Will can be a player," Daniel said, cutting her off.

"A player?" She was prepared for him to have lower expectations for Will but not to have impossible ones. "How exactly do you expect a child with cerebral palsy to play baseball?"

"I've done my homework," Daniel said calmly. "When I was ten, we had a kid with Down syndrome on our team. Will can definitely play ball if he wants to." He paused, narrowing his eyes as he looked at her. "His only limitation in this scenario would be, well, you."

Adaline drew back, her mouth falling open. "Me?"

"Now hold on." Daniel held up a hand. "I didn't say that to offend you, Addie."

"You could have fooled me," she snapped. "And my name is Adaline."

The corner of his mouth kicked up in a half smile, which made her madder for some reason. "Every child should be able to play ball if they want to, regardless of their abilities. I put more stock in a child's strengths than in their weaknesses."

Adaline shook her head as she tried to figure out what was

going on right now. She'd come prepared to fight for her son, but now she felt like the table had been flipped and Daniel was the one fighting for him and she was the bad guy somehow.

"Will has lots of strengths," Daniel told her.

She crossed her arms over her chest, mirroring his position. "I know that. He's my son," she said, defenses rising. "You haven't even known Will long enough to understand what he can or can't do. The last thing I want is some coach with a hero complex getting Will's hopes up, only to let them crash. Will has been through enough."

"Trust me, I don't have a hero complex, Addie… Adaline. And I'm not going to let Will get hurt. He can use a lightweight bat and a tee for hitting. Lots of kids his age still use a tee, so that's not a big deal. I can also assign a peer runner for the bases." Daniel's arms unfolded as he tapped out the accommodations on his fingers, his eyes lighting up as he thought through his plan for Will.

She listened, remembering how Daniel used to spend hours telling her about baseball strategies. She used to pretend to be interested just for his benefit, but really, she only cared about him.

"The Little League rules allow for disability accommodations. We just need to be creative," he said with a shrug.

"Wow," Adaline said quietly. "It sounds like you've put some thought into this." Adaline felt her carefully constructed walls begin to waver. Daniel had clearly done his research since yesterday afternoon, just to make sure Will felt included. The ideas could work, but trusting Daniel with her son was a risk. Regardless of Will's struggles, he was hopeful and more determined than anyone she'd ever known. He'd faced more challenges in his eight years than most people did in a lifetime, and yet, his faith was unwavering.

"Mom?"

Adaline glanced over her shoulder and smiled back at Will, who had returned and was watching their exchange with wide, excited eyes.

"What do you say, buddy?" Daniel stepped over and crouched down to Will's level. "Do you still want to be a Prairie Dog?"

Will looked at Adaline, hazel eyes pleading for her to say yes. "Can I, Mom? Can I really play?"

Adaline looked between her son and Daniel, side by side. Their similarities took her breath away. Both had almond-shaped eyes that looked green or brown depending on the lighting. Both had a shade of brown hair that resembled the color of clay earth.

"Addie?" Daniel asked. Then he lowered his gaze momentarily. "Sorry, old habits die hard."

Tell that to her heart. She looked away, pulse thundering in her ears. Was this a huge mistake? Or was God opening doors that never should have been shut? She nodded slightly. "Yes. It's okay with me."

Will erupted in a loud cheer that made her laugh.

"Great," Daniel said. "Practices are on Tuesday and Thursday evenings. The first game isn't until next month. I want the kids to warm up and get to know one another. They also need to learn the rules. Will isn't the only kid who's never played ball."

"Thank you," she said softly, pushing down her assorted feelings to navigate later when she was alone.

Daniel brushed the dirt from his knees as he returned to a standing position. "Don't thank me yet. Practice starts in ten minutes, and Coach Daniel runs a tight ship."

Despite herself, a smile tugged the corners of her lips. "Talking about yourself in third person?" she teased. "You know I'm a reading specialist," she said. "Grammar is important."

"If I recall, you're also a writer," he reminded her.

She shook her head. "Not really. Not anymore." And she didn't want to talk about herself. Their relationship needed to be strictly professional and focused on Will.

"Once a writer, always a writer, Addie." Daniel offered a meaningful look before turning to Will. "All right, buddy. Let's get you a uniform."

Daniel positioned himself behind home plate, watching as Carson helped Will get comfortable with the lightweight aluminum bat. The familiar scratch of metal cleats on concrete and the pop of balls hitting gloves created a rhythm that felt like coming home.

"All right, Prairie Dogs!" he called out. "Let's work on our basics. Pair up for warm-up throws. Will, you and Carson take the spot near first base." The lower angle would give Will better stability with his walker.

Daniel glanced at Adaline on the bleachers, watching every move he made. She'd trusted him with her son tonight, which was a huge deal, not just because of who he was to her. Daniel somehow thought Adaline struggled to trust anyone with Will. He could only imagine how tough things had been for her, raising a son with special needs alone after losing her husband early in their marriage.

"Remember, keep your eye on the ball," he called out, moving between the pairs, adjusting grips and stances. "Even major leaguers have to master the fundamentals. Tommy, rotate your shoulder back a little more," he told one of the older boys. "That's it." He headed toward Will and Carson.

Will was using a modified glove that was easier to maneuver, and Carson naturally adjusted his throws to accommodate his friend's position.

"Great job, Will!" Daniel encouraged as Will caught a throw. "See how he used his body to block the ball?" he asked the others. "That's exactly what we want to see, everyone."

Just like on his dad's farm earlier today, he felt a sense of peace here on this worn-out baseball diamond where he'd spent countless summers of his youth. Unlike so many places where he'd been since graduation, everything made sense in these familiar spots. Here, there were no failed business ventures, no disappointed investors and no eviction notices. Just the simple joy of teaching kids his own favorite pastime.

"Coach Daniel," Justin called from left field a few minutes later. "Can we practice hitting now?"

"Sure thing. Everyone circle up first." The boys jogged in, Carson sticking by Will's side as he used his walker. They all formed a semicircle around him. "We need to review how our practices will work and talk strategy so we're ready for our first game."

"But Coach Daniel," Tommy piped up, brows scrunched in worry, "won't Will slow us down when we have real games?"

Daniel caught the flash of hurt in Will's expression. It was brief and quickly masked by the kind of resignation that no eight-year-old should have to feel. Before Daniel could respond, Carson stepped forward.

"Will is super smart and he can do anything that I can. He just needs a little help sometimes, but we all do," Carson said.

Daniel was proud of the boy. "Carson's right. God made us different and that's a good thing. We're a team, which means my strengths cover your weaknesses, and your strengths cover mine. That's what makes a successful team."

What did he know about success? He'd gone off and wrecked every endeavor he'd ever attempted. Looking around at all the excited, optimistic faces of these little boys, he hoped this endeavor would be the end of his losing streak.

"But he's slow, Coach Daniel," Tommy continued.

Daniel couldn't blame the kid. Tommy only knew what he'd been taught. It was Daniel's job to teach a different kind of lesson. Crouching to put himself on the same level as the boys, he looked at each one. "During warm-ups, I noticed Will has an eagle eye. He can spot a bad pitch faster than any of you." He winked at Will, whose expression brightened. "And with the tee, his hit placement is going to be precise, which will be huge for us in a tight game."

Tommy looked skeptical. "Really?"

"Absolutely. Plus, having a peer runner means we'll essentially have an extra player on base. That's going to throw off the other team's strategy. Each inning, we'll have a different teammate designated as Will's runner. When Will hits, his runner will be ready to sprint. It's like having a secret weapon."

"Like a pinch runner in the major leagues?" Justin asked, catching Daniel's excitement.

"Exactly!" Daniel nodded. "And Will's going to be our dugout captain too. With his eye for the game, he'll help us track the opposing pitcher's patterns. That's how we'll know when to expect a fastball or a changeup."

"I can do that?" Will asked.

"You sure can. Plus, you and a couple others will help me manage our batting order and keep everyone focused. A team needs more than just players—it needs strategy and leadership too."

Justin raised his hand. "Can Will help coach first base? My cousin's team has a kid who does that!"

"See there? We're already thinking like a great team." This was one of the things Daniel loved and had missed about his hometown of Prairie. Small towns were naturally welcoming and understanding. They were like one big family, which came with positives and frustrations too. "We can position Will's walker right there at first. Just like with all the players, once I get an idea of Will's strengths, I'll assign him secondary roles." Daniel looked over at Will. "Sound good?"

"Sounds great!" Will said with unbridled enthusiasm.

"Will is really good at math," Carson mentioned. "Maybe he can help keep score some nights."

"Great thought." Daniel appreciated the boy's enthusiasm. "All right, Prairie Dogs, let's put all this teamwork into practice," Daniel called out to the team. "We're going to have three stations. Station one is bunting practice with me. Station two is batting practice with the tee." Everyone was going to use the tee today so that Will didn't feel singled out. "Station three is fielding practice. I'll blow my whistle and we'll rotate every fifteen minutes. Remember, baseball is about playing to everyone's strengths. The Yankees don't ask their pitchers to be their best hitters, and we don't need everyone to be good at the same things. We just need everyone to give their best. All for the glory of God, right?"

The kids cheered in agreement. Daniel glanced over at Adaline on the bleachers, her shoulders relaxed and a soft smile lining her lips now.

As the practice continued, the boys adapted and included Will. When it was Will's turn at the tee, Justin and Tommy cheered just as loudly for his well-placed bunt as they had for Carson's earlier hit to the outfield.

*Thank You, God.* Some part of Daniel had thought he'd fail miserably at coaching Little League baseball too. But tonight had gone even better than expected.

As practice wrapped up, Daniel tried to catch Adaline before she left. He wanted to reiterate his intentions for Will. Allowing him a spot on the team wasn't out of pity. Will would be an asset and he wanted Adaline to know that. Before he could make his way to the bleachers where she was collecting her things, however, Tommy's mother intercepted him.

"Coach Daniel?"

"Hello, Ms. Miller. How are you?"

"Please, Daniel." She waved a hand and laughed. "We've known each other since second grade. Call me Erica." She touched his arm lightly, a lipstick-coated smile spreading across her lips. "I just wanted to tell you how great you were with the boys this evening. Tommy is excited to have you as a stand-in coach."

"Thank you, Ms. Miller." He took a subtle step back, maintaining politeness but creating distance. "Milo told me what a good group they are."

She tilted her head to the side, winding her finger around a strand of hair. "Yes, they've all been playing ball together since preschool. Well, almost all of them."

Daniel guessed she was referring to Will. Milo would have made a spot for Will on the team too. Daniel knew that. He guessed Will just hadn't asked until now, inspired by his friend Carson. Daniel's gaze reached past Ms. Miller toward the bleachers, where Adaline was no longer seated.

"Well, I just wanted to give you a proper welcome back. I also wondered if you would like to have dinner this week. There's a new place downtown that I'm sure you haven't been yet."

"Oh. I appreciate the invitation," Daniel said, looking at her again and choosing his words wisely. "Unfortunately, when I'm not here on the field, I'll be spending my evenings helping my mom while Dad recovers from double pneumonia. I'm caring for the horses and managing the farm."

"Of course," Ms. Miller said. "How thoughtless of me.

We're all praying for Pastor Matthews. I think it's wonderful of you to drop everything and come home to care for your parents."

That wasn't exactly the truth. Everyone in Prairie assumed he'd returned out of the goodness of his heart just to help his family, but he wasn't as noble as they thought. He wasn't a small-town hero by any means, but closer to a failure and fraud. At least that's how he felt some days.

"Well, Coach Daniel," Ms. Miller said, regaining his attention, "I'll see you at church this weekend?"

Daniel shifted uncomfortably. "Perhaps." Daniel loved attending church, but his relationship with his father's congregation was…complicated. Once upon a time, everyone had thought he'd follow in his dad's footsteps, including himself. He'd earned their respect and had taken on responsibilities in high school. Then he'd lost his best friend in a car accident and he'd spiraled in a very public way.

Carlos was in a coma for weeks. Daniel had organized every prayer chain. His faith had heightened in some ways during that time. Daniel was certain that God was going to answer his prayers because Daniel was faithful. Daniel prayed scripture over his friend. He prayed every waking moment and he'd wholeheartedly believed. So when Carlos didn't pull through, Daniel short-circuited. He was hurt. Angry. Full of rage. He felt betrayed by God even.

He stopped attending church. Put his Bible under his bed to collect dust. He stepped down from assisting with the youth group. He also quit the baseball team at his school. His grades just barely squeaked by for the next year. His father tried to talk to him, but Daniel wouldn't listen to anyone—not until he ran into Adaline one day at the local park. She was a year younger than him and relatively new to his school. He'd seen her around, but they'd never spoken until that day when he'd been at his lowest point. She sat down beside him and offered him a piece of gum that felt like a lifeline. She was the first person to make him feel alive again.

Daniel's gaze searched the bleachers and the gate as Ms. Miller continued to talk.

"Well, perhaps a rain check for that dinner date once your father is feeling better."

Daniel nodded, but it wasn't the yes that she seemed to think it was.

"Great," she said, her smile returning. "I'll look forward to it." She patted his arm and then gestured to Tommy waiting for her by the gate. "Good night."

"Good night." By the time Daniel made it to the parking lot, Adaline was at her midsize SUV.

"Here, let me help with that," Daniel offered, carefully lifting Will's walker into the trunk.

The irritation radiating from Adaline was palpable. Had he done something wrong with coaching Will? Did she overhear Sarah Miller's invitation to dinner?

"Practice was awesome, Coach Daniel!" Will exclaimed, oblivious to his mom's mood. "Did you see how far I hit that last ball, Mom?"

"I did, sweetheart. You did a great job."

"I'm just so glad you decided to give him the chance," Daniel offered.

Adaline's head snapped up and her eyes narrowed. "Give him the chance? I always prioritize my son's needs."

"I only meant I'm glad you gave *me* a chance. To coach Will." The last thing he wanted to do was upset Adaline, which apparently, he'd already done. "I won't let you down."

"It's not me I'm worried about." Her tone was neutral as her gaze flicked toward Will.

"I won't let either of you down," Daniel clarified.

Adaline had always been good at masking her emotions. Only those who knew her best got access to the truth of what she was feeling. He had once been one of those trusted few. "We'll see about that."

"Can Coach Daniel come over for dinner this week? He probably knows all kinds of baseball tricks," Will said from the back seat.

Adaline visibly froze, her hand on the SUV door. For a moment, Daniel was transported back to the dinners she'd spent at his family's house. His mom had quickly bonded with Adaline when he first started hanging out with her. Anyone who could lift the burden from Daniel's shoulders even momentarily was welcome at their home, which meant his mom invited Adaline over on a near nightly basis, treating her just like a daughter. "I'm not sure, honey."

Daniel noticed that Adaline was avoiding his gaze. "When did you join the church, by the way?" he asked, recalling that his mother hadn't just invited Adaline to dinner. She'd also extended invitations to their church back then, which Daniel had blocked, suspecting it was just his mom's way of trying to turn him back toward his faith. He was still too mad at God for taking Carlos from him, though. No way was he stepping foot in any church, and neither was his girlfriend.

How could he have been so selfish?

"Last year." Adaline glanced over, finally meeting his eyes.

"Because of me," Will piped up proudly.

"Well, that's a story I'd like to hear," Daniel said, gaining a grin from Will.

Adaline sighed. "I'm afraid it'll have to be a story for another day. Right now, Will and I need to get home to prepare for bed."

Will's answering groan reminded Daniel of himself at that age. He'd never wanted the fun to stop back then.

"Good night," she told Daniel before dipping into the driver's seat.

"Night." He watched her close the SUV door, shutting him out. Reluctantly, he headed toward his truck. He'd reconciled with God a long time ago, but not with Adaline. Daniel didn't expect to pick up their romantic relationship where they'd left off, of course, but he'd love to be friends again. She still meant a lot to him. More than he'd allowed himself to remember.

# *Chapter Three*

"Dear God..." Will clasped his hands together on top of his Lightning McQueen comforter.

Adaline also folded her hands as she sat on the edge of his bed and bowed her head. It had been a big day for her son, thanks to Daniel.

"Thank You for this awesome day, God. And thank You for letting me join the baseball team, and thank You especially for Coach Daniel. He told Tommy all the great stuff about me that I didn't even know. Now Tommy is looking at me like I'm cool, which is pretty awesome."

Adaline smiled, cracking one eye open to look at Will.

"And thank You for my mom," Will continued. "She's the best mom ever, even when she's scared to let me try new things." Will opened his eyes and caught her watching him.

She quickly shut her eyes, feeling caught red-handed.

With a giggle, Will rattled off a few more thanks and requests in prayer. "God, please help Pastor Matthews feel better soon. Our assistant pastor, Pastor Jason, does a good job, but I really miss Pastor Matthews. Amen."

"Amen," Adaline echoed softly, leaning forward to kiss his forehead. Afterward, she tousled his hair with one hand.

"Mom?" Will caught her hand before she could stand. "Why don't you like Coach Daniel?"

Her mouth fell open.

"Is it because he accepted me on the team?" Will's forehead wrinkled the way it did when he was completing his homework, except it was her that he was studying. "Because I thought that was a good thing."

"What makes you think I don't like him?" She smoothed his hair back from his face, reminding herself to schedule a haircut for him next week. "I do like Daniel. In fact, I've always admired him as a person."

"Because he's Pastor Matthews's son?" Will asked.

Adaline shook her head. "I don't admire him because of who his parents are, no. I became friends with Daniel long before I ever went to Prairie Community Church." She tilted her head as she looked at her son and gave him a playful nudge. "You know that."

Will's grin stretched from one ear to the other. "Coach Daniel wants to hear that story about me inviting you to church."

She nodded. There wasn't much to tell. For years, Will had gone to church with her best friend, Beth, and Beth's son, Carson. And every Sunday when Beth brought Will home, he'd pitched the idea of Adaline coming with them next time until finally Adaline agreed.

"So, if you admire Coach Daniel, why don't you want me to like him?" Will asked.

Adaline sighed softly. She'd promised herself on the day that Will was born that she would never treat her son the way her parents had treated her: like an inconvenience. Her mother had left so long ago that Adaline barely remembered anything about her. And her father spent as little time as he could with her, letting the television parent her and prepackaged food feed her. Adaline wanted better for Will. She wanted the best for him, even if "the best" in this moment was Daniel Matthews.

"You know, Coach Daniel isn't married either, Mom," Will said.

Adaline felt her eyes widen. "And how do you know that?"

"Carson told me," Will admitted with a grin. "And I overheard Mrs. Peterson mention him at church last week. She said all the single ladies would be aiming to get his attention."

"Of course she did." Adaline stood and tucked the blanket around Will's shoulders. "Why are you telling me this anyway?"

"Because I can't keep you company forever, Mom."

She wanted to laugh but Will wore a serious expression. "Okay."

"One day, Will Harper is going to grow up and live on his own."

She hoped he did. That's why she worked so hard to give him all the therapy and resources he needed. "Will Harper, huh? That name sounds familiar." She tapped her pointer finger to her chin, pretending to think. "Wait. Isn't that your name?" she teased.

His grin stretched wide.

"Don't worry about me, sweetheart. I'll be just fine," she told him. "Now, time for sleep, my little baseball player."

She kissed his cheek and had almost reached the door when his voice stopped her.

"Mom?"

"Hmm?" She turned, feeling the weight of the day pressing on her own eyelids. She could guess that as soon as she lay down tonight she'd be out like a light.

"Just because you're a grown-up and a mommy doesn't mean you can't chase dreams too. Maybe Coach Daniel will let you play on the baseball team with me."

Adaline did laugh this time. "Baseball was never my dream, sweetie."

No, writing had been her dream. Daniel had reminded her of that earlier, which was interesting because she rarely thought of those long-ago dreams. The stack of notebooks in her bedside drawer held fragments of a dozen different stories that she'd stopped and started over the years, never feeling like they were worthwhile or good enough. Even if they were, single working mothers didn't have time to write books on the side. At least not this one.

After closing Will's bedroom door, Adaline retreated to her own bed and burrowed under her covers, remembering how that young, dreamy-eyed version of herself who'd planned to change lives with her writing had shriveled back into her shell after being dumped by Daniel. She hadn't made the best choices after her heartbreak. Instead, she'd finally accepted a date with a guy she liked but didn't love. After a brief courtship, she'd married Christopher and welcomed a beautiful boy into the world a short time later. While Daniel went off to find success outside of Prairie, she pushed her plans aside and focused on survival. For a while things had seemed like they would work out. Then she got the call that her husband had unexpectedly died.

Between physical and occupational therapy appointments, school IEP meetings and the constant juggling act of being a single working mother, the Adaline that Daniel had known faded into a warrior who took on the world for the sake of her son. She'd fought insurance battles and bone-deep exhaustion to make sure Will had the very best chance at succeeding with his disability.

She was a different person now. What would she and Daniel even talk about if they did have dinner? she wondered, staring up at her dark ceiling. The easy connection they'd once shared seemed like something from another lifetime. The bigger question loomed more heavily. If they sat across the table from one another, would Daniel notice Will's deeply carved dimples that resembled his own? Would he recognize their similar laugh or the way Will sometimes referred to himself in third person just like Daniel?

Rolling onto her side, Adaline closed her eyes. God was the author and finisher of all stories, and she trusted He had a plan in bringing Daniel back to Prairie. Just like He'd led Adaline to Prairie Community Church. The foolish lies she'd told as a scared teenager needed to be cleared up. Now that she was a Christian woman, Adaline knew she couldn't move forward in her walk with God much longer without telling Daniel, and Will, the truth. She didn't care if it brought the community's judgment on herself or ruined her reputation. What did concern her, however, was Will. How would he handle the truth when it finally came out?

Early on Sunday morning, Daniel followed the aroma of freshly brewed coffee into the kitchen, where his father sat at the table, looking stronger than he had in weeks. "Hey, Dad. Looks like you have some color finally returning to your cheeks."

His father's chuckle sounded strong as well. "Morning, son." His dad gestured to the coffeepot. "Your mother just made a fresh pot if you want some."

"I'd love some coffee." Daniel poured himself a full mug and settled across from his father, watching steam curl from their matching mugs.

"Star seems happy to have you home," his father commented, talking about Daniel's favorite horse. "She's always been partial to you." There was no trace of the pneumonia that had stolen his breath in the past weeks. "I can't tell you how much it means to me that you'd come help."

If his father only knew how close he'd been to complete

failure in Atlanta and how the thought of coming home had been tugging at him long before his mother's call.

"There is nowhere else I'd rather be right now."

His father lowered his gaze, his eyes briefly shiny. "Glad to hear it."

Daniel wondered if he should fill his dad in on all the failures in his recent life. He didn't want to worry him when he was sick. He just didn't have anything to go back to in Atlanta and he didn't want his parents to think him being here was a burden.

"Dad…"

"Good morning, Daniel." His mother rounded the corner already dressed in her Sunday attire, a long cotton dress paired with clunky leather boots. Roberta Matthews was a cowgirl at heart and, while you could sit her on the front pew as the pastor's wife, you couldn't make her wear heels. "What are you two chattering about?"

She leaned down to kiss her husband's cheek and then stepped over to do the same to Daniel's.

"Just telling Dad that he doesn't need to thank me anymore," Daniel told her. "As much as you both have done for me over the years, I would say yes to just about anything."

"Good to know! Then you won't mind taking me to church this morning," she replied. "Your father's still not quite up to it."

Daniel nearly spit his sip of coffee. He hadn't even unpacked his bags enough to locate a tie. More importantly, the thought of listening to the hushed whispers of his father's congregation was more than he'd bargained for when he'd gotten up this morning.

His mother's hand settled on his shoulder, gentle but firm. "Everyone has a past," she said, as if reading his thoughts. "You have nothing to be ashamed of."

The weight of those words settled in his chest. He knew she was right, but he couldn't help feeling shame for the way he'd turned on the church after Carlos died.

"Sometimes forgiving yourself is the hardest thing to do," his father added, taking a careful sip of his coffee. "Your mother shouldn't have to sit alone on the pew. I know I've already surpassed my quota of favors, but I'd appreciate it if you went with her, son."

Daniel nodded. "Of course. I can do that." He'd have to face the criticism sooner or later—might as well rip off the Band-Aid today.

His mother's face lit up as she poured her own cup of coffee. "Everyone will be so happy to see you. And you'll get to hear Pastor Jason preach. Jason's sermons are well thought out."

His dad cleared his throat, looking at Daniel's mother over his coffee mug.

On a laugh, she waved a hand. "Yours are too, sweetheart." She winked at Daniel. "Pastor Jason just brings a younger voice."

"God brings the voice and the sermons," his dad reminded her. Then he looked at Daniel. "Your mother's right. Jason is doing a wonderful job in my absence."

Jason had been one of the teens in Daniel's youth group once upon a time. Now he was standing behind the podium in the place that Daniel might have been if he'd handled Carlos's death differently and made better choices.

"I'm looking forward to seeing Jason in action," Daniel said. "What's the message going to be on?"

The way Daniel's father shared a glanced with his mom got his attention. "I believe the message is around the prodigal son," his father responded.

Daniel stiffened, second-guessing his agreement to go.

His dad quickly raised his hands in surrender. "As I said, God brings the voice and the message. I had nothing to do with the topic of today's sermon."

*Message received loud and clear*, Daniel told God as nervous laughter bubbled up in his throat.

"You know, son," his father said, "people often forget that the prodigal son's father ran to meet him while he was still a long way off. Didn't wait for him to reach the house and he didn't demand explanations. He just ran to embrace him the way any decent father would." His dad gave him a meaningful look. "Of course, that son had no choice. The livestock were eating better than him."

Daniel hadn't been eating with the livestock back in Atlanta, but he'd been getting tired of ramen. "I'll, uh, go change." He pushed back from the table, stood and turned to head down the hall.

"Your navy suit is pressed and hanging in your closet," his mother called. "I did it yesterday, just in case."

*Just in case.* The words echoed in his mind as he entered his old bedroom. Daniel had just heard a sermon on the prodigal son at the church he attended in Atlanta three weeks back. If he recalled the story's details correctly, the prodigal son had rehearsed his speech of repentance and had planned to beg for a servant's position when he returned home.

Daniel had rehearsed a speech of his own over the years, imagining the day he would walk back into his father's church. He'd wanted to wait until he had something to show for all the time he'd been away. No amount of success would erase the way he'd treated those in the Prairie Community Church, however. Yes, Daniel had lost a friend and it was understandable that he'd been upset, but he'd said hurtful things that he couldn't take back. He'd lashed out at people who were only trying to help. Instead of receiving their love, Daniel had pushed them away.

Today was the day of reckoning.

Stepping into his childhood bedroom, Daniel stopped and took in the pressed navy suit hanging in his closet. How many Sunday mornings had he worn a suit like this one, standing beside his father in the church foyer and greeting parishioners? How many times had he envisioned himself behind the very pulpit where his father stood every Sunday?

Instead of grabbing the suit, Daniel grabbed the hanger that held a pair of slate-gray pants and a casual button-down linen shirt. He wasn't his father's mini-me anymore. As he dressed, he heard his parents' voices carrying down the hallway.

"Roberta, would you mind saving me some of that coconut cream pie from the fellowship hall? A man can't live on chicken soup alone."

"Doctor's orders," Daniel's mother reminded his dad.

"Doctor's orders didn't say anything about pie," his father called back.

Their familiar bickering brought a smile to Daniel's face. Some things never changed, even when everything else did. Maybe that's what coming home was really about: finding that solid ground again. The prodigal son of the Bible had to lose everything to realize what he'd had all along. Perhaps the same was true for Daniel.

Turning to the mirror, he finished buttoning the top buttons of his shirt in the mirror and took a long look into his own eyes, hazel like his mother's. Coming home was hard. He'd be the talk of the town for a moment, but not for the first time. With a sigh, he headed out of his childhood bedroom, prepared to attend his childhood church. And to see his high school sweetheart, who his mother had continued to invite to church even after Daniel broke up with her. From what Daniel had heard, his mom continued inviting Adaline to dinner too. Adaline needed a family and just because Daniel abandoned her didn't mean his parents would.

"You didn't wear the suit I laid out for you," Daniel's mother said, meeting him at the front door.

"This is more comfortable."

His mom patted his chest. "Well, you look handsome."

"Thanks. See you in a little bit, Dad," he called to his father somewhere in the living room. Then he grabbed his keys and followed his mom down the porch steps.

"All the single women will be noticing you and wondering if you're the answer to their prayers for a good husband," his mom said. "And the women my age, of course, will wonder if you're the answer to their prayers for a good spouse for their daughters."

Daniel's mouth suddenly went dry and once again he second-guessed his agreement to attend church service. The only woman's reaction he cared about this morning was Adaline's. Would Addie see him as an answer to her prayers?

# Chapter Four

"Mom, this is embarrassing!"

Adaline ignored Will's whispered objections as she smoothed his cowlick into place. The familiar scent of old hymnal pages and lemon furniture polish wrapped around them as they sat on the third row of pews along the left-hand side as she had every Sunday morning for the past year.

"Good morning, dear," came a voice from behind them. Mrs. Henderson, silver haired and well-meaning, leaned forward with a slight smile. "How are you managing, sweetie? It must be hard raising that precious boy all by yourself."

Adaline forced a smile. When Adaline had first started coming with Will, Mrs. Henderson's weekly comments had gotten under Adaline's skin. But God was working on Adaline's heart. "We're doing just fine. Thank you for asking."

"Of course, dear. You're so strong. I don't know how single mothers do it." The older woman's voice carried just enough volume to reach the nearby pews, gathering unwanted attention and looks from fellow parishioners. "He needs a father figure, you know." Mrs. Henderson lowered her voice just a touch to give the appearance that she was trying to be private. Even Will was listening though. She reached out to pat Adaline's right shoulder. "You're on my daily prayer list, sweetie."

"One can never have enough prayers in their corner," Adaline said, reminding herself that the sweet silver-haired woman didn't mean any harm. "You're on my prayer list as well, Mrs. Henderson."

The older woman sat up straighter and looked around to see who had overheard.

Adaline felt immediate conviction. She was still pretty new at being a Christian, but if Mrs. Henderson looked even a tiny bit embarrassed, she was remorseful. *Forgive me, Lord*, she silently prayed.

"Mom?" Will tugged her sleeve a moment later. "Why does Mrs. H talk about us like we're broken?"

At eight, Will was already too perceptive. Adaline had tried to shield him from the weight of others' opinions, but in a small town like Prairie, privacy was a luxury they couldn't afford.

"Jesus was the only perfect one. Aside from Him, we all have nicks and bruises. Everyone has a crack here and there, but you're right. We're not broken, sweetheart."

Will had been putting more weight into what others said lately and asking innocent questions that cut straight through Adaline's defenses. Questions like "Why did Daddy die?" and "Did Daddy love me?"

He was talking about Adaline's late husband, who everyone just assumed was Will's father. Christopher knew the truth though and he'd been fine to keep it between them. He'd loved Will like his own and he'd loved Adaline as well.

Then there was Will's latest question: "Can we get a new dad from somewhere?" This had made her laugh out loud even though the tears pressed behind her eyes.

"And just where exactly would we get a new dad, Will? From the farmers market on Saturday?" she'd asked.

Even though they'd laughed together, the void in Will's life was clear. He hadn't had enough years with her late husband to even remember how it felt to have a father in his life.

He longed for what his friends had, and what she couldn't be for him.

As the choir started singing their opening hymn, Will's attention shifted to the back of the sanctuary. From the corner of her eye, Adaline noticed Will's face brighten the way it did when his best friend, Carson, walked into the room, or when he heard the tune of the ice cream truck careening down their street.

"Coach! Coach!" Will called out, waving enthusiastically, momentarily forgetting where they were.

"Shh." Adaline patted his hand down, feeling heat creep up her neck as heads turned in their direction once again. The heat wasn't just due to embarrassment. It was also because Daniel Matthews was walking down the center aisle with Mrs. Matthews, looking more handsome than she recalled ever seeing him. He also looked...more uncomfortable than usual.

Daniel's eyes immediately found Will and he returned a wave.

"Mom," Will whispered, "I feel bad for Coach Daniel."

Adaline furrowed her brow. "Why, sweetheart?"

"Well, because I know how it feels when everyone stares." Will's matter-of-fact tone broke her heart. "Kids stare and talk about me all the time. Sometimes they don't let me sit with them at lunch because I'm too different."

Working at the same school Will attended, Adaline had witnessed this firsthand. "I'm sorry that happens to you."

Will shrugged. "Coach needs a friend. Can we invite him to sit with us?"

"Coach Daniel is sitting with his mother." Adaline tipped her head as Daniel passed by and took a seat on the front pew, his shoulders visibly tense.

"Coach!" Will called again.

Daniel glanced back and grinned. Then his eyes slid to

meet Adaline's. He mouthed a silent hello that sent her heart racing.

*God, what are You doing?* she prayed. She didn't expect a response to her silent prayer, but a Bible verse popped into her mind. *For I know the thoughts I think toward you, saith the Lord, thoughts of peace, and not of evil, to give you an expected end.*

Trust didn't come naturally to Adaline. It was something she had to work at, growing up in her household. But sitting here, watching Daniel supporting his mother and interacting with her son, she felt that old flutter of possibility.

Halfway through Pastor Jason's sermon, Adaline became aware of Will squirming beside her.

"Mom," he whispered loudly. "Mom, I have to go to the bathroom."

Adaline pressed a finger to her lips, but there was a quiet desperation in his eyes. With a nod, she helped Will stand and steady his walker. Then they made their way toward the outer aisle. Adaline was acutely aware of the eyes in the congregation following their slow progress. There was no hurrying Will though. She'd learned that long ago. Rushing might lead to a fall and that would bring the whole sermon to a standstill. If there was one thing Will had taught her, it was patience. And love.

They headed out of the front entrance of the church and stepped over to the door to an adjacent building with Sunday school classrooms and restrooms. Adaline started to follow Will into the boys' bathroom until he stopped abruptly and looked at her.

"Mom."

Right. He was getting too old for her to fix his hair in church or to help him in the bathroom. He wasn't too old, however, to keep his voice quiet in the sanctuary. Adaline offered a small nod. "I'll wait out here for you. Don't forget to wash your hands."

Will gave her another look. There'd been a point when Will had needed help with everything. He was becoming more independent, which was a good thing. And she was doing her best to step back and allow him to shine.

"Adaline!" Tammy Richardson stepped up beside her. "How are you?"

Despite Tammy's consistent kindness, Adaline felt her guard slowly rise the way it did with any interactions with other parents. People were naturally curious about Will's disability, which had sometimes come out wrong in the past. The comments still did at times, but Adaline's skin had thickened.

"Hi, Tammy. I'm good. How have you been?"

"Oh, busy-busy. Brian is into every sport these days. I feel like I live my life on a ball field of some sort." Tammy laughed. "I don't think there's any child more active than him." Her smile faltered mid-sentence, as if she'd suddenly remembered who she was talking to. The change was subtle but unmistakable, and Adaline felt that familiar pinch of pain in her chest. Another reason her guard went up around parents.

"You must be very proud of him," Adaline said, giving Tammy a warm smile.

"I am. You must be proud of Will as well," she echoed back, but Adaline noted the lack of sincerity. Tammy probably believed there was nothing to be proud of regarding Will. Maybe that was a harsh thought, but in Adaline's experience other parents didn't understand what a victory it was sometimes to even take a step. To stretch another inch. Not when their child was making home runs on the ball field.

"I am proud of Will," Adaline said. "He's doing great in school."

They both turned to the restroom door as it swung open and Will attempted to push through.

Tammy's son, Brian, stepped up behind Will and held the door. "I got it, Will."

"Thanks, Brian," Will replied, looking grateful.

So he could accept help from a friend but not her. Noted, she thought, taking that as a victory as well. Kids wanted their independence and Will was no different.

"Well, we'd best get back to the service," Tammy said, reaching for Brian's hand. "Hey, I know I've invited you before, but you should reconsider joining the Single Mothers Support Group. It meets here every Friday evening. Childcare provided."

"We can hang out together," Brian told Will, overhearing.

Adaline had dodged invitations to join the group before, but her excuse had always been that she didn't like leaving Will. Now it seemed, Will wanted to be left.

Brian tugged Tammy's sleeve. "Mom, I forgot to tell you. Will joined the Prairie Dogs team. I'm one of his peer runners."

Tammy's brow line lifted. "Oh? I've never heard that term before."

"Neither had I," Adaline offered. "Coach Daniel has been really good to Will."

"Well, welcome to the team, Will," Tammy said. "I guess you'll be living on the ball field this season too," she told Adaline. "And maybe on Friday nights, you'll join me here for Bible study and sweet treats."

The assistant pastor's voice carried clearly through the sanctuary as he read from Luke 15:20: "'And he arose, and came to his father. But when he was yet a great way off, his father saw him, and had compassion, and ran, and fell on his neck, and kissed him.'"

Daniel tried to focus on the scripture instead of his spiraling thoughts. His shirt collar seemed too tight around his neck and he had the urge to undo the top button. His mind couldn't help making mental comparisons between himself and the prodigal son. He was even worse than that son.

He'd raged at God. He'd left his morals and values for a time and he'd rebelled hard. Then when his grieving had subsided, he'd felt unworthy of the life he'd always dreamed of. He'd told himself, and God, that the ministry was his father's calling, not his. Full of shame, he'd left his hometown with self-derived dreams of corporate conquests, turning his back on everything and everyone in Prairie.

If he were meant to be a pastor, he wouldn't have had a crisis of faith. He would have been steadfast, even when he was grieving his friend. Instead, he'd concocted plans for a life that would be impressive and mask his shortcomings. Instead, he'd stumbled at every roadblock and, sitting here on the front pew, he was no better off than he'd been nine years ago.

Pastor Jason caught Daniel's wandering gaze as he preached. "'The son said unto him, "Father, I have sinned against heaven, and in thy sight, and am no more worthy to be called thy son."'"

It was similar to the prayer that Daniel had prayed in Atlanta: "God, I am no longer worthy. Maybe I never was."

"'It was meet that we should make merry, and be glad: for this thy brother was dead, and is alive again; and was lost, and is found.'" Pastor Jason looked out on the congregation. "He was given grace by his family. Haven't we all made mistakes? I know I have. And we all deserve grace. If Jesus can give it to us, so much more should we give it to our neighbors. Shall we pray?" he said, bowing his head.

The congregation mirrored his gesture and all eyes closed.

"And, Lord, we lift up Pastor Matthews in prayer," Pastor Jason prayed. "We pray that Your will be done in all things and that You would be with Pastor Matthews and his family, comforting them and wrapping them in Your healing love. Amen."

When the prayer concluded, Daniel opened his eyes and braced himself for the inevitable.

"So good to see you, Daniel."

"How are things in Atlanta?"

"Staying long this time?" Each conversation was a delicate dance around the truth. Perhaps he'd been lying to himself for so long that even he wasn't sure what exactly the truth was.

"I'm happy to be home," he said honestly. Even though most didn't know how horribly his endeavors had gone, there was still the subtle judgment from some over the choices he'd made.

"Adaline!" his mother called out suddenly, waving an arm to flag Adaline down. "Would you and Will like to join us for Sunday lunch? Just like the old days."

Daniel met Adaline's eyes, noting the way her body tensed.

"Oh, that's very kind of you, Mrs. Matthews," Adaline replied, though Daniel could hear the hesitation in her voice. "But Will and I should probably—"

"Please, Mom?" Will interrupted. "I want to hear more baseball stories from Coach Daniel."

"Another time, maybe," Adaline said gently.

Daniel felt a pang of disappointment that surprised him.

"Thank you again for the invitation, Mrs. Matthews. Please give Pastor Matthews my best wishes for a speedy recovery."

"Will do," Daniel's mother said before being roped into conversation with another member of the congregation.

Daniel wanted to follow Adaline and Will out, but his mother tugged on his arm, looping hers with his and pulling him into the next conversation.

It took fifteen minutes to extract themselves from the post-service social obligations: questions about his father's condition, offers to help with the farm, gentle inquiries about Daniel's plans. When they finally made it to the parking lot, Daniel exhaled a breath and noticed Adaline's SUV was still parked under the old oak tree.

His mother followed his gaze. "Adaline is usually long gone by this point. You should go check on her." His mom winked and grabbed the keys from Daniel's hand. "I'll wait in the truck."

His mother made an art out of issuing commands without actually asking the other person to do anything and subtly implying that the thing she wanted was the other person's idea. If she had wanted to go into business, she would have been a shark.

"Sure. I'll meet you at the truck in just a minute." Daniel walked over to where Adaline stood beside her vehicle. Will was already buckled in his car seat but looking restless. "Everything okay?"

"Car trouble," she said on a sigh, working to pop the vehicle's hood. "It's been slowly dying on me. I was hoping to make it another month or two before it gave up completely."

Daniel peered down at the engine. "Can your dad take a look at it?"

Adaline's expression dimmed, and Daniel immediately knew he'd said something wrong. "My dad moved into an assisted living facility last year."

"I'm sorry, Addie. I didn't know."

Her gaze jumped from the engine to him at the sound of her nickname. She didn't correct him this time though. She didn't even seem to mind. "It's okay. As you know, Dad isn't the social butterfly, and people don't really announce things like that. It's not like a wedding or a funeral. Moving into assisted living is more of a life transition."

Daniel remembered Adaline's father as a quiet man who'd always seemed more comfortable with engines than people. Adaline had never been particularly close to him, but Daniel imagined if her father needed assisted living care, the divide between them was likely widening.

"Dad's arthritis wouldn't allow him to work on my engine anyway, and I'm not sure he'd remember how to fix it," she added.

"Well, I guess you have no choice then, do you?" Daniel asked, surprising himself with his boldness. "Now you have to join us for lunch." He cleared his throat, suddenly worried Adaline would take his comment wrong. "Or, I can skip lunch with my parents and I can look at this now."

Adaline shook her head. "No. I don't want you to miss dinner with your parents."

"Mommm, I'm hungry!" Will's voice carried through the open car window.

She looked at Daniel again and relented. "Okay. Thank you. I guess a home-cooked meal would be good. Your mom's cooking sounds delicious, actually."

"Great." Daniel gave Will a thumbs-up. "I'll work on your car later and see what I can do," he told Adaline.

"You're our hero today, I guess," she said, closing the SUV's hood and turning to face him. "You've been so wonderful letting Will join the team, and now this. I don't know how to thank you."

Daniel met her eyes, seeing the exhaustion of carrying

everything alone. "I could never do enough to make up for the past. But I plan to try."

The moment stretched between them, charged with memories. There was a spark of something that had never fully faded after all these years.

Maybe it wasn't too late for Daniel, but he was far from being the hero she and everyone else thought he was. At least the prodigal son returned home without pretenses.

"There's something I need to tell you, Addie."

Her smile fell just slightly. Before she could ask the obvious question or let him explain, Will pushed open the vehicle's back door.

"Don't forget about me," he called from the back seat. "A growing ball player has to eat."

"Indeed, he does," Daniel said, helping Will out of the SUV and steadying him behind his walker. Will wasted no time pushing forward in the direction of Daniel's truck across the parking lot.

"You sit up front with Daniel," Daniel's mother told Adaline. "I'll take the back seat with my buddy Will."

Adaline shared a look with Daniel as she slid into the truck beside him. There were so many questions in her eyes. Questions he'd answer before the day was over because suddenly his silence felt like a lie that needed to be ripped off like a Band-Aid.

## *Chapter Five*

Adaline couldn't eat another bite. Setting her fork down, she sighed happily, wishing she could retreat to the couch for a nap.

"Mom, why don't you cook like this?" Will asked.

Adaline knew he didn't mean to hurt her feelings, but the question hit on her constant worry of not being "enough." As a single mom, she always felt like she was falling short.

"Your mama is too busy doing all the other things," Mrs. Matthews answered, sitting across the table from them. "I'm retired, Will, so I have all the time in the world to cook." She winked at Adaline. "And it does my heart so good to watch you eat and enjoy it." She slid her gaze to Daniel. "And to watch you enjoy it too. I love having my son home."

"Well, if you feed me like this too often, Mom, I might never leave," he teased.

"Fine by me." Mrs. Matthews reached for Pastor Matthews's hand. He still had lingering pallor from the double pneumonia that had kept him bedridden for weeks, but he'd sat through the meal, laughing at Will's lively conversation.

"Would you like me to help clean up?" Adaline asked, already beginning to gather the plates nearest to her.

Mrs. Matthews shooed her hands from the plates and looked at Will with a conspiratorial smile. "My buddy Will would probably like to help clear dishes, wouldn't he? Helpers get a cookie on the flip side."

Will nodded excitedly.

Adaline immediately envisioned broken dishes scattered across the Matthewses' kitchen floor. Will's cerebral palsy affected his fine motor skills, and his enthusiasm often outweighed his coordination. She opened her mouth to politely decline, but Mrs. Matthews seemed to read her mind.

Leaning in closer, Mrs. Matthews appeared to reveal a secret. "The truth is, I have butter fingers. These dishes are plastic if you couldn't tell. I grew tired of chipping my best china a long time ago."

Adaline's shoulders relaxed at her sides. Mrs. Matthews had always been thoughtful about Will's needs, never making a big production of accommodating him but simply ensuring he could participate fully. Daniel must have learned to do the same from her.

"Now," Mrs. Matthews continued, standing to begin clearing the table, "Daniel, why don't you take Adaline back to her vehicle and see if a good jump start will do the trick?"

Adaline highly doubted it would be that simple. Her SUV had been making concerning noises for weeks. Sometimes it just needed an extra nudge for the engine to turn over though, and hopefully that would be the case this afternoon. She didn't have the funds for a new car right now.

"Take your time," Mrs. Matthews told them. "Me and Will might even clean up some carrots to feed the horses later."

"Yes! Can we really feed the horses, Mrs. Matthews?"

"Of course we can, sweetie. Star loves carrots as much as you love my chocolate chip cookies."

Adaline ignored the familiar tug of anxiety that came with leaving Will in someone else's care. She rarely left him with others, but Mrs. Matthews had always been patient and understanding about all the ways that Will's cerebral palsy affected him. She was the grandmother Will needed in his life, which only made Adaline feel guiltier. She accepted as many invitations from the Matthewses as she could, but if Mrs. Matthews knew Will was her own flesh and blood, they'd probably insist on seeing him more often.

Adaline smoothed Will's hair as she prepared to leave. "Listen to Mrs. Matthews and behave."

"Mommm," he said, just like he had earlier when she'd started to follow him inside the bathroom.

Mr. Independent, and that was a testament to his maturity. He was growing up fast and, seeing him sit across the table from Daniel, he was looking more and more like his father every day. Her gaze moved to Daniel, recalling his boyish features from before he'd left for college. He was a man now, complete with the faint hint of stubble growing in along his angled jawline and shoulders that had broadened from the lanky teenager she remembered.

"If the jump start doesn't work, I'll call Andrew Neally," Daniel told her.

Adaline's relaxed shoulders tensed again. "Oh, I'm not sure I have the funds for a mechanic right now. If my car can't be started, we can just tow it to my place. Will and I can carpool to the school for a while." She felt awkward giving insight into her financial circumstances but, being a single mother who worked at the local school, it wasn't hard for anyone to guess that she was barely making ends meet.

"Oh, don't you worry yourself," Mrs. Matthews said, overhearing the conversation. "Daniel would be more than happy to drive you and Will to and from school every day if necessary. Wouldn't you, son?" She looked at Daniel with that motherly expectation that dared him to argue. "He's not too busy."

Daniel reflected awkwardness now. Instead of financial assumptions, Adaline guessed it was about his availability. He'd been a businessman in Atlanta, but what was he doing now? Did he have a job to get back to? Was he working remotely to care for his father? Was he unemployed? The questions suddenly buzzed in Adaline's mind. He'd wanted to tell her something earlier. Was it about his circumstances?

"Yes, of course." Daniel cleared his throat and gave a nod.

"No," Adaline said. "I wouldn't want you to wake early just for us."

"Nonsense," Mrs. Matthews replied. "Daniel has been up with the chickens lately anyway. He can drive you and Will to school and return to finish up the farm work here. He's also helping us with the medical appointments, of course." She patted Daniel's shoulder. "It feels just like the old days, having you home to help with everything."

Mrs. Matthews made a shooing motion. "Now go on, you two. Don't you worry about me and Will. We're going to have ourselves a good old time."

Daniel led Adaline out to his truck and walked around to open the passenger door for her. "Sorry about that," he said.

Adaline had rarely dated in her adult life, but most of the men hadn't opened doors. The thought to do so had probably not even crossed their minds.

"About what?" she asked as she climbed in.

"About having an overbearing mother who hasn't realized yet that I'm no longer a kid."

Adaline smiled. "Now that I'm a parent, I completely understand why she acts that way. I do the same with Will."

"It's the hardest job in the world, right? Being a parent." He didn't wait for an answer. Instead, he closed the passenger door and jogged around the front of the truck.

Parenting was hard, but it was also the most rewarding responsibility that God had ever given her. Guilt landed heavily on her shoulders. Daniel was also a parent. God had blessed him too, but he had no idea.

Would he hate her if he discovered the truth? She'd always consoled herself about keeping the secret by telling herself she couldn't tell Daniel because he wasn't in Prairie. He'd chosen his big dreams over her. She'd rationalized her silence by convincing herself she didn't want him to return out of obligation. The truth was more complicated though.

After being abandoned by her mom and neglected by her father, trust didn't come easily for Adaline. Daniel broke that trust, shattered it, and when she'd found out she was pregnant, panic set in. What if Daniel tried to take Will from her? What if the Matthewses took Will? All her fears came to life and she wasn't willing to risk the only family she had. Her late husband seemed like the answer. Their marriage protected Will because no one questioned the paternity. Christopher loved Will, but he didn't want to take him from Adaline. He just wanted her as a wife. He took care of her and Will and she'd loved him in her own way—never the same way she loved Daniel though.

"You're awfully quiet over there," Daniel said as he drove. "Something on your mind?"

"The past," Adaline said honestly.

The truck's engine hummed softly as Daniel navigated the familiar streets of Prairie, past the old Miller farmhouse with its peeling white paint and the corner market. Adaline pressed her palms against her jeans, trying to still the nervous energy that had been building since he first walked into church this morning. Since he returned to town.

"Good past or complicated past?" Daniel asked.

"Both, I guess."

"Fair enough." He slowed for the stop sign at Maple and

Third, the same intersection where they'd shared their first kiss. The memory came out of nowhere. She hadn't been expecting the kiss that day. She'd had dinner at the Matthewses' home and he was driving her back to her house.

"Do you remember—" they both started to say simultaneously, then stopped and laughed awkwardly.

"You first," Daniel said.

"No, you."

The truck idled at the stop sign longer than necessary. Daniel's hands gripped and released the steering wheel repetitively, reminding her of the way he'd done the same in their youth. It was a nervous habit. One she used to offer comfort to by reaching out and giving him her hand. They didn't have that kind of relationship anymore, though.

"I was going to ask if you remember how we used to drive around for hours, just talking," he said finally, removing his hand from the steering wheel and holding it out, palm up.

Adaline glanced at his hand, noticing the calluses on his palm before he took hold of the steering wheel again. She doubted he got them working in business. As a teenager, she recalled how much he'd loathed being asked to help with his father's horses and shoveling out the barn. She wondered if his attitude had changed toward those chores now. He seemed genuinely happy to be back in Prairie, which surprised her.

"We'd put maybe ten miles on the odometer," Daniel continued, "but somehow manage to cover the entire county."

Adaline laughed quietly, remembering all too well. "Your dad's Chevy only picked up the country radio station," she added.

"And you pretended like country music was your nemesis," he teased.

"Well, it's not my preferred music genre," she said, keeping her tone of voice warm.

Daniel's eyebrows rose as he finally pulled through the intersection. "If I recall, you always sang every word to those songs as we drove."

The easy banter between them felt nice. But underneath it, Adaline felt the weight of everything unsaid pressing against her chest.

"What were you going to say?" Daniel asked. "Before we both started talking at once?"

Adaline watched out the window as the town of Prairie rolled past. "I was going to ask if you remember what you said to me the night before you left for college." She glanced over in time to see the muscles of his jaw bunch and soften.

"Of course I do. I said nothing would change. I told you that I'd come back for you every chance I got."

"You said you loved me," she added. She had loved him too. That was the thing that hurt the most.

They drove in silence for nearly a mile.

Finally, Daniel cleared his throat. "I meant it, Addie," he said quietly. "But life…" He trailed off, shaking his head. "I didn't recognize myself by the time I went to college. I wasn't the man I thought I was. I turned my back on everything I'd always believed in. I didn't know who I was anymore. How could I love you when I didn't love myself?"

"So you broke up with me," Adaline said. It wasn't a question.

"It felt like the right move." He glanced over. "The next thing I knew, my mother told me you were engaged to a guy you barely knew," he said.

As if that justified what he'd done. "You told me not to wait for you. So I listened." She shrugged and lowered her head, remembering the fear that consumed her back then. Time wasn't on her side and panic mode had set in when she realized she was pregnant.

"I was a fool, Addie," he said. "I have a lot of regrets. That's one of the biggest."

"Telling me you love me?" she asked.

"No. Letting you go."

Before she could respond, the steeple of Prairie Community Church came into view. Adaline's SUV sat exactly where she'd left it, looking defeated in the empty parking lot. The past was suddenly replaced with her present day problems: car trouble, tight finances and single motherhood.

"She looks like she's seen better days," Daniel said, pulling up along the vehicle.

Adaline managed a weak smile. "Be nice to Lilly. She's gotten me and Will through a lot."

"Lilly? You named your car?" Daniel cut the engine and looked at her fully for the first time during the drive, his hazel eyes serious.

"She's a member of the family," Adaline teased. "Me, Will and Lilly." Maybe it was strange, but Adaline would take all the family she could get.

Daniel cleared his throat. "Adaline, what I was trying to tell you earlier, after church—"

"Daniel, don't." The words came out sharper than she intended. Her emotions were already raw and she didn't want to cry right now. She just wanted to fix her car and go home. "Please…not right now."

Confusion drew his dark brows inward. "Why not?"

Adaline's hands shook as she reached for the door handle. Whatever Daniel wanted to tell her, it couldn't be worse than the secret she was hiding from him. Her late husband wasn't Will's birth father. Will's father was sitting right here, close enough to touch, and completely unaware that he'd left behind more than just her nine years ago.

She knew it was wrong not to tell Daniel, but fear paralyzed her. “I just need to focus on getting my car started,” she said, climbing out of the truck. “One crisis at a time.” That’s how she’d lived the last nine years.

Daniel got out too, grabbing the jumper cables from the truck’s bed. “Fair enough, but I do want to talk. Sooner than later.”

Sweat slid down Daniel’s back as he leaned over the open hood of Adaline’s SUV and inspected the engine. He’d rolled up the sleeves of his linen shirt, wishing he’d taken the time to change clothes before heading this way. He also wished he’d taken shop class in high school. Each failed attempt to coax life back into the stubborn engine only made him feel more like a failure.

“Come on,” he muttered under his breath, checking the connections one more time. The battery terminals were clean, the cables were properly attached and his truck was running strong. Everything should have worked. But Adaline’s car refused to cooperate.

He tried turning the key in the ignition one more time, listening to the clicking sound that yielded nothing. Not even a hint that the engine was considering turning over. Daniel wiped his hands on his already-stained shirt and stepped back. He lowered the hood and faced Adaline.

“I’ll take you and Will to and from school this week, and to ball practice. During the day tomorrow, I’ll get Andrew Neally on the case.” He paused, wishing Adaline didn’t look as defeated as he felt right now. “I wish I’d taken your dad up on learning how to fix a car when we were dating.”

Adaline’s expression softened, and she offered him a small smile. “It was your senior year. You had other priorities, like getting into college.”

“Let’s be honest. All I wanted was to hang out with you.”

Up to then, he'd spent his youth following in his father's footsteps, memorizing scripture and preparing for a life of ministry. Until Carlos died the summer before his senior year. That was the turning point for Daniel, and not a good one. He'd slowly gotten back to center, but this past month felt like another turning point in Daniel's life, this one positive.

"So, what time should I pick you and Will up tomorrow?"

"I appreciate your help, Daniel, but I can't ask you to—"

Daniel cut her off, his voice softer than he intended. "You aren't asking and you heard my mother back at the house. She didn't ask me either. She pretty much demanded that this is what would happen."

"Okay," she said with a small smile. "We'll be ready at seven o'clock. Will is going to be so excited to ride with Coach Daniel. He might insist that you walk him to class just to show you off to his friends."

"I wouldn't mind," Daniel said, and he meant it completely. The thought of being someone Will looked up to filled him with warmth. He'd be honored if that were the case. All his friends from high school had become fathers while he was away chasing broken dreams in Atlanta. They had a contentment that came from building something meaningful and lasting. He felt that void lately, especially when he looked at Adaline and saw the quiet strength that came from not just surviving, but thriving. He doubted she thought she was thriving, especially now with her car troubles, but he saw it. She woke up every day with purpose. He admired her.

Daniel gestured toward his truck. "Let's get out of the heat."

After climbing back into the vehicle and cranking the engine, Daniel sat for a long moment, grateful for the blast of air-conditioning cooling his skin. As the truck idled, he and Adaline turned to one another at the same time.

"Addie, I need to tell you—"

"Daniel, there's something—"

They both stopped and blinked in surprise at one another as they spoke simultaneously.

"This keeps happening to us," Adaline laughed.

Daniel gestured for her to speak first. "You go ahead."

Adaline shook her head. "You first."

Daniel was grateful for the go-ahead. He couldn't keep going on, letting others believe he was this noble, self-sacrificing son who was only back home to selflessly care for his parents' farm and offset the workload on his mom while his dad recovered.

"I didn't come home because my dad was sick," he said quickly. "I mean, I did come home for that reason, but it's not the way everyone thinks. I'm not a good son."

Adaline's brow furrowed, but she quietly waited for him to continue.

"I want to be a good son. A good man. I want to be here for my parents and help Mom take care of Dad, but I didn't drop everything to do that. The truth is, my business career was a bust," Daniel continued, the admission making it hard to meet Adaline's eyes. "I've been failing miserably for the past two years. Everything I touched has turned to dust. I lost clients, made terrible decisions and basically proved that I had no business being in business." He pulled in a deep breath but he still felt like he was suffocating. "The shame and regret has been keeping me awake at night and I need you to know who I am."

He stared out the windshield at the church where he'd grown up listening to his father preach countless sermons about grace and forgiveness. "I've been thinking about coming home for a while."

"Why didn't you?" Adaline asked quietly.

"Pride, I guess. Every time I nearly made the decision, I'd get a tiny nibble in my career, and I'd convince myself that my big break was right around the corner." He shrugged. "It never was. All I got was more tired and homesick. When Mom called to ask me to come help with the farm, well, I couldn't get here fast enough. I used my last dollar on gas. I'm not the success others think I am."

Adaline reached across the center console and placed her hand over his, her touch gentle and warm. "You're being too hard on yourself. Maybe you didn't just come home to help, but you are helping. That's still true. You're a good son, Daniel."

Her words meant more to him than she could know, and he wanted to believe her. "Thank you. But I wasn't a good boyfriend. I wasn't even a good friend. You've been through so much, Addie, and I haven't been there for you. Being here these past weeks and seeing you has made me realize just how much you've gone through. Alone."

Adaline's expression shifted as she seemed to process what he'd said. "It hasn't been easy, but I haven't exactly been alone. Your parents have offered a lot of support. The church has been amazing to me too, even before I started attending."

"I'm not surprised. I'm so glad to be back in this town. I've missed the people here." He searched her gaze, not saying that he'd missed her the most.

She gave him a long look. "Sounds like you wouldn't have returned if you'd found what you were looking for. If your business ventures had gone well, you'd have stayed."

Daniel was tired of bending the truth to make himself look like a good guy. He'd spent too many years crafting a false image of success, and he was done with the pretense. "Maybe. If things had worked out for me, I guess I might have continued down that path." He pulled in a long breath and exhaled. "I wouldn't have been happy though—I know that. I also know that I would have dropped everything to come home and help with the farm and Dad's care."

Adaline nodded. "See? You are a good son. You come home for those you care about." Suddenly, she looked upset, but he wasn't sure why. She pulled her hand away from his, the loss of her touch leaving him feeling cold and empty.

What just happened? "What did you want to tell me?" Daniel asked.

Adaline shook her head. "It's not important."

Something told Daniel that it was though. He knew her too well to press. He just needed to wait until she was ready, which he didn't mind doing. Now that he was back in Prairie, he was in no hurry to leave.

## *Chapter Six*

"Today was the best day ever, Mom," Will said later that evening, his gap-toothed grin stretching wide. "Mrs. Matthews let me help her make chocolate chip cookies, and I didn't drop a single one. Then we took carrots to the horses, and Star ate right out of my hand!"

Adaline settled on the edge of his bed. "That does sound like fun."

"Mrs. Matthews said I was the best helper she's ever had," Will continued, his voice animated. "She said I could come back anytime I want and help with the horses. Do you think we can visit again next Sunday?"

"We'll see." Adaline tried to hold her smile in place, but she'd let worry creep in since earlier in the day when her car had refused to start. The earlier conversation with Daniel also weighed on her mind. Daniel's admission wasn't horrible, but it highlighted the fact that Daniel would have chosen success over her. She'd needed him and he hadn't come home, but he did return for his parents. They were his family and she and Will were not.

She couldn't hold that against Daniel. He didn't know Will was his son. She'd hidden that fact from him by marrying her late husband. Daniel thought he was an awful person just because he'd fumbled a few things in life, but she'd done so much more.

"Mom, are you sad about our car?"

Adaline blinked out of her thoughts and looked at Will, who was watching her. He was so perceptive. She really needed to do a better job of masking the things that troubled her. A child his age shouldn't be burdened with adult problems. "Oh, honey, I—"

"You don't need to be upset," Will interrupted, his voice taking on the serious tone he sometimes used when he was trying to be grown-up. "Remember what Pastor Matthews always says? God works all things for good for those who love Him."

Adaline's heart swelled with so much love. At eight years old, Will had such unwavering faith that things would work out. She hadn't been raised in the church. When she was growing up, she remembered often feeling hopeless. Then she'd met Daniel.

Reaching over, she smoothed Will's dark hair, the same color as Daniel's, away from his forehead. "You are absolutely right. You have such a good heart."

Will beamed. "Maybe the good side of our car troubles is that Coach Daniel will take us to and from school all week. Won't that be so cool? I can't wait to tell Carson that Coach Daniel is our friend."

She loved seeing Will so excited about Daniel, but it also troubled her. He'd only come home because he had no other choice. Yes, he'd come home to help his parents too, but he was struggling in his career. He wasn't secure and, in some ways, he seemed lost. What if Will bonded with Daniel and then Daniel left again? What if he broke her son's heart the way he'd broken Adaline's once upon a time?

"We can't inconvenience Coach Daniel too much," she said carefully. "He's very busy taking care of his parents and the farm."

"But he said he wouldn't mind," Will protested. "And Mrs. Matthews said Coach Daniel would be up early anyway for chickens. And the horses."

"I know, sweetie, but we don't want to take advantage of his kindness." Adaline stood and moved toward the light switch. "Now, it's time for prayers. You need to get some sleep."

Will obediently folded his hands and closed his eyes. Adaline closed her own eyes and listened as his sweet voice filled the quiet room.

"Dear God, thank You for today's sermon. Thank You for the good food that Mrs. Matthews made and for letting me help her bake cookies. Thank You for the horses and for Star eating carrots from my hand. Please help Pastor Matthews to get better soon so that he can preach again. Not that Pastor Jason is boring or anything. And please help my mom be happy again."

Adaline's eyes popped open, her heart skipping a beat. She waited for Will to finish settling into his pillow before speaking.

"Amen," Will said.

"What did you mean by that last part, sweetie?" Adaline asked.

Will looked up at her with those earnest hazel eyes, more green than usual tonight. "About what?"

"About helping me be happy again. What makes you think I'm not happy? I'm very happy." Adaline walked back over and returned to sitting on the edge of his bed. "I have a beautiful, smart, healthy son who I love more than anything in the world. I have a great job working at the school. I have wonderful people in my life who care about us."

Will's expression grew uncharacteristically sad, and he

seemed to consider his words carefully. “But you don’t have the kind of friend that other moms have.”

“What do you mean?”

“The husband kind,” he said quietly. “Like Mr. and Mrs. Johnson, and Mr. and Mrs. Peterson. You don’t have that kind of friend.”

Adaline’s heart clenched. “I have everything I need. You and I make a pretty great team, don’t we?”

Will didn’t look entirely convinced, but he nodded. As she stood to leave the room again, Will called out to her. “Mom?”

She turned back, waiting patiently for him to say whatever was on his mind.

“Mrs. Matthews said I can have my birthday party at her house, if you say yes.”

Adaline had been trying to decide what to do for him for his upcoming ninth birthday. They usually had small celebrations at home with cake and a few friends from school, but attendance had been sparse the past couple of years.

“Why would you want to have it at Mrs. Matthews’s house instead of our own home?”

“A farm birthday would be so cool! We could feed the horses and maybe play in the barn. And Coach Daniel would automatically be there since it’s his parents’ house.” His voice rose with enthusiasm. “How cool would it be for me to have the coach at my birthday party? All of my friends will be so impressed.”

Will had always struggled to make friends due to his cerebral palsy. Some children were kind, but others were either overly cautious around him or, worse, dismissive. The fact that Will believed the location or having Coach Daniel there would make others want to attend broke Adaline’s heart.

“Please, Mom? Can we do it?”

The party would mean more interaction with Daniel and

more opportunities for Will to become attached to someone who might leave again. But she could see how much it meant to her son, how his face glowed with the possibility of finally having a birthday party that made him feel special.

"I'll think about it," she said finally. "We can talk more about it later. For now, you need rest. You have school tomorrow. Good night, sweetheart."

She flipped the light switch and closed his door behind her, then paused in the hallway. The weight of the day suddenly felt heavy on her shoulders. Leaning against the wall, she closed her eyes and pulled a deep breath into her lungs.

She could feel that familiar stirring in her spirit that she'd learned to recognize as God's gentle nudging. He was doing something. He was weaving circumstances together in ways she couldn't fully understand yet. It wasn't coincidence that Daniel was back in town and suddenly coaching Little League when Will was becoming interested in playing. Her car had passed inspection last month, but now it wasn't even cranking. Mrs. and Pastor Matthews had always been good to Will, but they'd never offered to host his birthday party. Until now. It felt like God was slowly revealing pieces of a puzzle that might work together to make a complete picture.

It was time to tell Daniel the truth. Long past time. The secret of Will's true paternity had only grown heavier over the years. It would complicate everything. She knew that, but she trusted God would walk beside her the way He always had. Daniel was wrong; she'd never done any of this alone. God had been there with her, despite her secrets and lies.

Would Daniel be as loyal? Would her own son? Eight years was a lot of missed birthdays. This year, for Will's ninth birthday, she'd do the right thing. She'd give him the gift of truth and hope he didn't hate her for it.

* * *

As promised, Daniel pulled into Adaline's driveway at 7:15 a.m. on the dot. He'd been up since five thirty anyway, feeding the chickens and checking on the horses before grabbing a quick shower and coffee. The farm routine was coming back to him more easily than he'd expected, muscle memory from his teenage years. He didn't recall enjoying the farm chores as much back then as he was now though. The manual work felt good to his hands and freed up space in his mind where he could ponder and problem solve, and feel God's presence.

Daniel had barely parked in Adaline's driveway when Will burst through the front door with his walker leading the way. The boy moved with determined steps, navigating the front porch with practiced ease. Behind him, Adaline hovered over him, her expression guarded when she acknowledged Daniel. He'd tried to be honest with her yesterday and it had definitely changed the air between them. He just wasn't sure of the reason because her words contradicted her body language.

"Coach Daniel! I told my mom you'd be here right on time, and you were!" Will said.

Daniel came around his truck to help Will with his walker, lifting it into the truck bed while Adaline assisted Will into the back seat. "Morning, Will. You ready for school?"

"Yes! I can't wait to tell everyone that Coach Daniel drove me to school." Will's gap-toothed grin was infectious, and Daniel found himself smiling despite the tension radiating from Adaline.

"Morning, Addie," Daniel said as he climbed into the driver's side next to her.

"Good morning." She only offered a polite nod while avoiding his gaze. The contrast between how she'd treated him just twenty-four hours ago and now made it clear that even though she'd told him he was a good son and good man, she thought less of him knowing he'd failed at adulthood thus far.

After backing out of the driveway, Daniel put the truck in Drive and listened to Will's excited chatter all the way to school. Adaline remained silent, her jaw set in a way he remembered from high school when she was upset.

"Adaline," he said during a lull in Will's run-on conversation, "I hope what I told you yesterday didn't—"

"It's fine," she interrupted, her voice clipped.

It clearly wasn't fine. "I've been gone a long time, Addie. I never wanted to return to Prairie until I made something of myself. I wanted to be able to impress everyone when I came home." He'd wanted to impress her. It wouldn't have made ending their relationship right, but at least it wouldn't look like it was all for nothing.

Adaline folded her hands tightly in her lap. "The Daniel I knew never cared what others thought."

Daniel flinched. "He always cared what you thought though."

She looked over and raised a brow. She didn't need words for him to know what she was thinking. If he cared so much, why had he broken up with her?

Daniel pulled into the school's parking lot and parked in the nearest accessible spot for Will. "Addie..."

She was already pushing her door open and walking around to help Will get out.

"Coach Daniel, can you walk me inside?" Will asked. "Please? I want to show you to my teacher and my friends!"

Adaline's response was swift and firm. "Coach Daniel needs to get going with his day, Will. I'll walk with you."

"But Mom—"

"No buts," Adaline said. "Thank you for the ride, Daniel."

"Of course." He lifted Will's walker out of the truck bed and placed it in front of Will, watching as Adaline helped him stabilize on the sidewalk. The routine was clearly practiced, efficient, and it struck Daniel how much effort went into Will's daily life. Morning routines, school drop-offs, evening homework sessions. When did Adaline get to turn off the role of single parenting and be a woman? Did she still write? "Addie..."

"Adaline," she replied sharply. He saw her quick inhale and exhale and then she softened her tone. "We'll be ready for pickup at three thirty. We'll meet you under the breezeway."

"Okay. I'll be waiting." Daniel offered a smile that she didn't see because she wasn't looking at him anymore. She was actively avoiding looking at him.

Will glanced back over his shoulder every few steps as they headed toward the school's entrance. Daniel wished he could walk the boy inside. At least someone thought he could do no wrong.

Once Adaline and Will were inside the building, Daniel reluctantly got back into his truck and drove to meet Andrew Neally at the parking lot. Andrew was already parked beside Adaline's SUV when Daniel arrived, his head under the hood.

"She's seen better days," Andrew called out, straightening and wiping his hands on a rag. "Engine's shot, transmission's slipping and the electrical system's giving me fits. Honestly, Daniel, it would cost more to fix than the car's worth."

"Poor Lilly," Daniel muttered as his heart sank.

"Lilly?" Andrew asked.

Daniel smiled at the thought of Adaline naming her vehicle. "Send me the bill please."

"You sure? This ain't gonna be cheap," Andrew said, signaling the tow truck to hook up Adaline's car.

"I'm sure." The coaching job was pulling in a little bit of

money that he didn't need since he was staying with his parents right now. Adaline had enough on her plate. He owed her at least this much.

After Andrew left, Daniel used his father's key to enter the church. His dad had asked him to pick up some items from his office, but as Daniel walked into the empty sanctuary, he found himself pausing to look around. Growing up, this place had been his second home as well as his prison. Every pew held memories of sermons he'd sat through and youth group meetings he'd attended. The weight of expectations and missed opportunities pressed down on him like a physical force. He'd borne them as long as he could until Carlos's death.

"Daniel?"

Daniel turned to see Jason Miller, the church's assistant pastor, approaching from the podium where he'd been working. Jason and Daniel had both grown up in church and attended youth group with Carlos. They'd both lost a friend, yet Jason hadn't spiraled like Daniel. Instead, Jason's faith had grown stronger.

"Jason, hey." Daniel walked over to shake Jason's hand, genuinely pleased to see his old friend. "I wanted to catch up with you yesterday, but the after-church chitchat got out of hand."

Jason laughed knowingly. "Tell me about it. I was caught in it myself. Mrs. Henderson cornered me for twenty minutes about the church potluck schedule." They shared a comfortable laugh, but then Jason's expression grew more serious. "You know, Daniel, I feel like I'm standing in shoes that should have been yours."

"What do you mean?" he asked even though he knew exactly what Jason meant.

"As the pastor's son, you were the one everyone thought

would be behind this podium someday. I was the one always getting in trouble, remember?" He shrugged. "God works in mysterious ways, I guess."

"Agreed." Daniel couldn't help feeling the sharp sting of regret over his choices. God had more in store for him than he'd allowed. Daniel had stubbornly blocked every blessing God had wanted to give him because he was too proud. Too stubborn. Scared. "He certainly does."

Jason patted Daniel's back. "Well, I'm anxious to know. Tell me about your career in Atlanta. Business world treating you well?"

Daniel forced a smile and heard himself starting to spin the familiar tale about how well things were going. The words came easily after years of practice, but halfway through his rehearsed response, a small voice inside his mind whispered for him to stop. "I'm sorry." He paused mid-sentence and stared back at Jason with a blank expression.

"You're sorry? For what?"

Telling the truth hadn't done Daniel any favors with Adaline yesterday, but neither had omitting it all these years. "I was lying just now."

Jason's eyebrows rose. He gestured for Daniel to take a seat next to him on the pew. "Go on."

"My career bottomed out months ago," Daniel continued, the words tumbling out. "I didn't even enjoy what I was doing. I jumped from one thing to another, but there was no passion. No fulfillment. I'm financially broke, and honestly, the sermon you preached yesterday about the prodigal son hit way too close to home."

Jason stood and grabbed the notebook where he'd been working on next Sunday's sermon. "I'm hungry," he said, matter-of-factly. "Want to grab a bite to eat? On me, of course.

It's the least I can do for the guy who steered me back in the right direction when I swerved out of the lines as a teenager."

Daniel recalled how he'd invited Jason to youth group every chance he'd gotten during his sophomore and junior years. "Burgers at the Ark?"

"Is there anywhere else to get a burger in Prairie?" Jason joked.

The Ark was a local diner that had been serving the same menu for thirty years. A lot of things changed, but this old diner never did. Over the next hour and burgers and fries, Daniel laid out every detail of the last decade.

"Since you're going to be home for a while," Jason said toward the end of the meal, "why don't you help out with the youth group? Our youth pastor is leaving for college in the fall."

Daniel nearly choked on a French fry. "After everything I just told you, you're offering me a job?"

Jason shrugged. "You didn't tell me anything I haven't heard from others. Everyone has stuff in their past. It's about what's in your heart."

Daniel was hit with just how much Jason had matured and grown over the years. "You're not standing in the spot where I should have been. You're exactly where God wants you." And Daniel was so proud of his friend. He gave his head a slight shake. "But I don't know, buddy. Teenagers are hard to figure out. And returning to the same position I was aiming for in high school seems like a step backward, to be honest. It'll be like I haven't advanced at all since leaving Prairie."

Jason laid money down on the tray with the bill. "Jesus washed feet, and that wasn't a demotion from sitting at the table with His disciples. All I'm asking is that you take this opportunity into your prayer life and talk to God about it. See what He says."

Daniel nodded. “I can do that.”

Jason stood and extended his hand. “God likes to use our mistakes and turn them into our mission. After Carlos’s accident, you needed someone. You pushed us all away, but the right person would have refused to let you.”

Daniel froze, gripping his friend’s hand.

“Maybe you can be that right person for a teenager one day.”

The thought gave Daniel goosebumps. “I’ll think about the job.”

“Good. I’ll pray for you.”

As Daniel walked back to his truck, he felt a sense of peace he hadn’t experienced in a long time. He had a lot to take to God in his quiet time this evening: the youth pastor position, his feelings about Adaline, his uncertainty about the future. Jason was right about Daniel needing support after Carlos’s accident. He’d shut down and everyone had let him, thinking he just needed time. If Daniel could help a kid like himself one day, that would be enough to make all his mistakes worthwhile.

Or most of them, at least.

# *Chapter Seven*

Adaline's fingers gripped the cool metal railing of the chain-link fence surrounding the baseball diamond as she watched Daniel coach the Prairie Dogs during one of their weeknight practices. Her mind wanted to hold onto resentment and anger, but her heart wouldn't let her. He was out there giving those children his complete attention and he looked like there was nowhere else he'd rather be.

She watched Daniel kneel beside Will with his walker, demonstrating how to hold the bat. She'd imagined Will having a father so many times over the years, someone who understood sports and could teach him the things that she couldn't. She wanted Will to have a father who wouldn't walk away the way her own mother had when she was young. Having a parent willingly turn their back on you was a pain that she didn't want for Will. Her son had already endured his share.

She wanted to believe Daniel would be the father Will needed, but her mind kept wandering to Sunday afternoon's conversation. Daniel had been so honest about his failures and his shame. He'd also told her about all his reasons for returning to Prairie, which had confirmed her worst fears. He was here because of his father's illness, but he was only staying because he'd run out of options. What did that mean for Will? There was an undeniable growing attachment between Daniel and Will. But what if he suddenly got his life together? Would he leave again and break her son's heart? *Their* son's heart.

From her position at the fence, she wondered how things might have been if she'd told Daniel the truth nine, almost ten, years ago. Would he have returned? Would he have chosen to stay? Would they have built a life together? Or would he have confirmed her fears by abandoning her or taking their son?

In hindsight, marrying a man she knew had a crush on her to cover up her pregnancy with Daniel was a bad idea. She knew Christopher though. He was a good man and without a doubt, she knew he'd never abandon her or Will the way Adaline's mother had done to her. She knew he'd support them and that was enough. He'd offered her stability and family, which was something she'd never had.

When Chris himself died unexpectedly at twenty-two, just two years after she'd married him, she'd been devastated—not just by the loss of her husband, but by the cruel irony of it all. She'd married him for security, and he'd left her a widow with a young son and crushing medical bills.

"What's wrong?" Beth asked from the other side of the fence as she approached. "Are your car troubles the reason for the long face?"

Adaline looked up and waved at her friend. "Among other things." Since her car was still out of commission, Adaline had texted Beth earlier to ask if she'd mind taking her and Will home after tonight's practice.

"Such as?" Beth asked, joining Adaline on the bleachers.

Adaline gestured toward the field, where Will swung the lightweight bat at the ball being pitched to him. The sound of metal rang out and Daniel tapped Will's peer runner, sending the child racing toward first base. "Will loves this so much. I just worry about him getting his hopes up."

"About baseball?" Beth asked.

"About everything. I mean, you know how kids can be. Sometimes they build things up in their minds. I don't want him thinking he's the next Babe Ruth."

Beth chuckled. "Carson has already claimed that title," she said sarcastically. "Somehow I suspect Coach Daniel is really what you're worried about though."

Was Adaline that obvious? "I'm not sure what you mean."

"Come on, Adaline. I know the history between you two. I also noticed the way your whole demeanor changed on Sunday morning when he walked into the sanctuary. And Will talks about him constantly." Beth's voice softened. "Whatever happened between you two is in the past. Don't let it affect Will. Let him play ball and fantasize about the big leagues. It's fine."

Adaline wasn't sure how to respond. Her relationship with Daniel wasn't fully in the past and it did affect Will, more than anyone knew. Instead of replying, she turned her attention to the field and watched as Daniel high-fived Will when his peer runner successfully made it to second base. The pure joy on her son's face was unmistakable.

"I used to fantasize about being a world-famous author, you know," she told Beth.

"What?" Beth elbowed her arm. "You never told me that."

"Well, not a famous one, really. I just wanted to write books that others loved to read."

Beth grinned. "Is that still your dream?"

Adaline stared at Beth blankly. "Are single moms allowed to dream?"

Beth laughed as if Adaline had just told a joke. Then she laid her hand on Adaline's back. "Oh, honey. Single mothers are not only allowed to have dreams—they need to have them." She cleared her throat. "And there's nothing wrong with having a little crush on the Little League coach either."

Adaline whipped her head to look at her friend. "As you said, Daniel is part of my past. He's a friend and that's all."

Beth held out her palms. "Okay, okay. But we do need to revisit that book-writing thing. Maybe over coffee? The boys can play on their tablets together."

"That would be nice. If my car is working again by then," she muttered.

"Maybe Friday night?" Beth suggested.

Adaline hesitated. "Maybe next Monday. I have plans on Friday, I think."

Beth looked intrigued. "A date?"

"No." Adaline pulled in a deep breath. "The Single Mothers Support Group at church. Tammy has been inviting me for months. I think maybe I should give it a try."

Beth elbowed her friend again. "Wow. There's something different about you these days, Adaline, and I like it." She followed Adaline's gaze toward center field, where Daniel was huddling with the players. "I hope the changes last."

Adaline did too. For her sake and for Will's.

When practice was over, Daniel walked Will to the fence where she was standing, both of them grinning and covered in dirt. Will's cheeks were flushed with exertion and happiness, and Daniel looked more relaxed than she'd seen him since he'd returned to Prairie.

"Mom, did you see? I hit the ball three times!"

Laughing, she nodded. "I saw, sweetheart. You did great."

Daniel stopped a few feet away. "He's a natural athlete. Good instincts and a great attitude. You should be proud."

"Oh, I am." The words came out more stiffly than she intended. Crushing on the Little League coach was not on her list of priorities. But, as much as she'd wrestled with the nudging in her spirit, she did prioritize telling him that he was a father.

"Addie, do you think we can talk? Just for a minute?" Daniel asked.

"Sure." Something about his expression worried her. "Will, stay here with Mrs. Peterson while I talk to Coach Daniel, okay?"

"Okay, Mom." Will leaned heavily on his walker, tired from practice, but still grinning.

They walked a few steps away from the crowd of parents and children, stopping near the dugout.

"Are you kicking him off the team?" Adaline asked nervously when he took too long to begin the conversation.

"What?" Daniel retracted his head. "Of course not. He's a good addition to the team."

Relief poured over her, followed by confusion. He'd already made his confessions about his career on Sunday afternoon. "Then what is it?"

"I've been thinking about our conversation," he began. "I can see that it bothered you, and I want you to know that I understand why."

Every muscle in Adaline's body tensed. "Oh?"

"The thing is, I've been running from this place, from my responsibilities, from expectations, from you, for so long that I forgot what I was running toward." He met her eyes directly. "Maybe coming back because I had no choice was exactly what I needed. God has a way of bringing us back to where we belong when we're too stubborn to see the path on our own."

There was such sincerity in his voice that it broke her heart. This was the Daniel she'd fallen for in high school. The Daniel who had looked past all her defenses and had seen the girl she'd been even when she was doing her best to hide. Daniel had so much hurt inside of him back then and he still did, she realized. The difference was, now he was trying to face things head-on instead of running.

"I wanted to tell you that I'm not sorry I'm here. I could get a job offer tomorrow and I don't think I'd take it."

"No…? I'm just worried about Will. I don't want him to get hurt," she said quietly, the words slipping out before she could stop them. "He's attached to you already."

"I don't want to see Will get hurt either," Daniel replied immediately. "Addie, that kid of yours is special. The way he approaches everything with such determination and joy, I mean, it's inspiring. I would never purposely do anything to hurt him…or you."

*But you already have*, she thought.

"I know you wouldn't mean to, but sometimes people leave, and children don't understand that it's not about them."

Daniel's expression grew serious. "Are we still talking about Will?"

Adaline felt the familiar sting of tears press behind her eyes, but she blinked them back. "I've got to go. It's a school night," she said, stepping back toward where Will was waiting. "Beth's taking us home this evening," she said before Daniel had a chance to offer. She didn't want to take advantage of his kindness, and she needed space to organize her thoughts right now. And her emotions. "Will has homework, and it takes a while for his body to relax," she explained.

"Right." Daniel looked down at his feet. "I should turn in early too. I've had a hard time getting to sleep lately. I've had so much on my mind."

"Me too." She wanted to just tell him. She wanted to tell Daniel the truth right here and right now.

"Do you think you'll ever forgive me for being young and immature? For being a fool?" he asked.

Her mouth fell open. "Daniel..."

"If I could I'd do things a lot differently, Addie. And who knows? Maybe we would have made a home run in the game of love." He gave her a sheepish grin. "Cheesy, right?"

"I like cheesy," she said, her heart racing. "I've already forgiven you, Daniel. I forgave you a long time ago."

Hope flickered in his expression.

"I just... Trust is hard for me, and I just can't forget," she whispered. "I wish I could."

"Slow down, Mom. Otherwise you'll be laid up in bed like Dad," Daniel told his mother as she bustled around with an energy he hadn't seen since before his father's illness. She was practically beaming as she pulled out notebooks and began making lists, her excitement over Will's upcoming birthday party infectious despite his own complicated feelings about the situation.

"I can't believe Adaline agreed to let Will have his ninth birthday party here," his mother said as she wrote "barn cleaning" at the top of her list. "It's going to be absolutely wonderful. We haven't had children running around this farm in years."

Daniel couldn't help but smile. "You're really going all out for this, aren't you?"

"Of course I am. This little boy deserves the best party we can give him." She looked up from her list, eyes sparkling. "Daniel, I'll need you to clean out the barn and get it ready for the festivities. Make sure there are no loose boards or anything dangerous. And we'll need to prepare the horses. I want all the children to be able to feed them apples and carrots safely. You know Star likes to nibble fingertips when she can."

"Mom, it's a kid's birthday party, not a county fair," Daniel said with amusement.

She waved a dismissive hand. "Nonsense. We're also going to need a piñata. Do they still make those baseball-themed ones? And I'm planning to make a cake from scratch. Maybe that chocolate cake with the peanut butter frosting that you always loved. Oh, but what if someone has a peanut allergy? I better stick to basic vanilla."

Daniel watched her scribble in her notebook. "You don't have to do all this. I'm sure Adaline would be happy with something simple."

"I'm doing this for Will." His mother paused in her writing and looked at him with a soft smile. "Daniel, that little boy reminds me so much of you at his age. The way he gets excited about the horses, his determination despite all his challenges, that mischievous glint in his eyes when he thinks he's being clever." She tapped her pen against the paper thoughtfully. "You wanted a party on the farm for your birthday at that age too. Do you remember? You begged us for weeks to let you have all your friends come feed the animals and play in the barn."

Daniel did remember, although the memory felt distant and hazy. "I guess I did, didn't I?"

"You were so excited that day. Your father let you stay up late helping him set up games in the barn, and you insisted on personally introducing each of your friends to every single animal on the farm." His mother's expression grew wistful. "Time goes by so quickly. It feels like yesterday, but here you are, all grown up and helping with another little boy's farm party."

The parallel struck Daniel oddly, but he couldn't quite put his finger on why. "Speaking of helping, Pastor Jason asked me to consider helping with the youth group at church."

His mother's eyes widened. Daniel could see her fighting the urge to jump with joy. "Oh, son, that's wonderful. The church needs good leaders, especially with the youth, which you seem to be quite good at, I've noticed."

Before Daniel could respond, her expression shifted to something more businesslike. "Before I forget, your father asked me to send you into his office when you got back from ball practice. He wants to talk to you about something."

"Any idea what he wants?"

She turned back to her party planning. "All he said was to send you to his office when you returned."

"I returned twenty minutes ago," he pointed out, "and you've been rambling on about a nine-year-old's birthday party since I walked through the door. If it was urgent, you probably would have mentioned it sooner."

"Go on, smart aleck." His mother made a shooing motion toward the hallway. "Let me finish my planning in peace."

As Daniel headed down the familiar hallway toward his father's office, he recalled taking this exact path ten years earlier, his palms sweaty and his heart pounding as he'd prepared to tell his father that he had gotten into Emory Business School and was declining the seminary school he'd planned to attend since he was twelve years old. It was hard to believe ten years had passed so quickly. And in those ten years, he'd started and failed a half-dozen business ventures. And Adaline had brought a whole person into the world. A person who apparently reminded his mother of Daniel at that age.

Daniel stopped in his tracks. For a moment, his mind tried to connect the dots. He'd been gone for ten years. Will was turning nine years old. That meant Will had been conceived right around the time Daniel left for college. He'd known that Adaline had married quickly after he'd ended things, but he hadn't actually considered just how soon she'd become pregnant after their breakup.

"Daniel? Is that you out there? Come on in, son!" his father called, hearing Daniel in the hallway.

Daniel stepped forward and entered his father's office. "You look healthier every time I see you, Dad," he said, though he noticed his dad was still pale. "Mom said you wanted to see me?"

"I did. Have a seat, son."

Daniel settled into the same chair he'd occupied during that difficult conversation a decade ago.

His father slid the ever-open Bible in front of him to the side and faced his son directly. "It's good to have you home, but as you said, I'm doing better. I can't ask you to give up your life and stay in Prairie forever. I called you here because I want to give you my full permission to leave if that's what you need to do."

Daniel was taken aback. "Dad—"

"I know Jason asked you to help with the youth group," his father continued. "And while I appreciate the gesture, I don't think that's wise. The group needs consistency, not someone who might be leaving again in a few months." His father leaned back in his chair. "I can bring in other help for the farm and church duties. Mrs. Henderson's nephew is looking for work, and the church board has been discussing hiring a second part-time assistant pastor."

"Dad, hold on just a minute." Daniel folded his hands on the desk in front of him, choosing his words carefully. "The truth is, coming home and helping out with the farm and the baseball team is the best thing that's happened to me in a long time. I've been wanting to return for years, but I just didn't know how."

"You didn't know how to come home?" His father looked perplexed. "Coming home is always an option. There's no need for a reason."

Daniel had felt like he needed one though. "As for the youth group, I've given it a lot of thought and I want to do it. In fact, I'm grateful to have an opportunity to serve. I think I have a lot to offer."

"I know you do, son." His father stretched his hand across the desk. "Welcome to the Prairie Community Church team. You've grown into a good man, son. A God-fearing man."

Daniel shook his father's hand firmly, overcome with gratitude for this second chance.

"Well, since you'll be staying, I guess you'll earn your keep by continuing to muck the barn."

Daniel chuckled. "I guess that's better than eating with the pigs," he said, referencing the prodigal son story. They talked a while longer and then Daniel got up.

"Good night, Dad." As he left the office and walked back toward the kitchen, the mathematics returned to his mind. Ten years ago, he'd left Prairie and broken up with his first love. And now Adaline's little boy was turning nine years old. A boy with the same brown hair and hazel eyes. A child who had the same off-kilter smile that Daniel saw in the mirror every morning. And the same love for baseball that had defined Daniel's own childhood.

"Uh-oh," his mother said as he reentered the kitchen, looking up from her party planning. "Your talk with your dad must have been about something serious. You look like you've just seen a burning bush or something."

"No, it was a good talk," Daniel managed, though his voice sounded strange to his own ears.

"Then what's the matter?"

Daniel's mind raced with possibilities that he'd never allowed himself to consider. There was no way that Adaline would keep such a monumental secret from him though. If Will was his child, she would have told him. Adaline was a good person. She always had been. Daniel didn't know her late husband, but there was a good chance he had brown hair and a love of baseball too. Who didn't love America's favorite game after all?

"You okay?" Daniel's mother asked.

"Yeah." Daniel nodded, pushing the thought away. Adaline was better than that and he felt guilty for even suspecting it. He'd be a blessed man to have a son like Will, but that wasn't the case.

# *Chapter Eight*

Adaline's thoughts were conflicted as she sat in the front seat of Daniel's truck heading toward the baseball diamond. Daniel had been faithfully picking them up each morning for school and driving them to baseball practices every Tuesday and Thursday night as promised. But where there had once been easy conversation and tentative smiles, now there was a careful politeness that felt like walking on eggshells, which she understood was mostly her fault.

He'd been trying to express his feelings for her the other day and she'd shut him down by telling him she'd forgiven but would never forget. It was a defensive move, a way to put up a wall and keep him at arm's length. Her sins were so much greater than his and she didn't want Daniel professing his love again when she knew deep down he'd change his mind after he found out the truth.

"Mom, I can't believe my birthday party is this Saturday!" Will said, his small voice hurdling Daniel's noisy truck engine. "Coach Daniel, are you sure it's okay to have it at your parents' farm? I mean, I know your mom said yes, but I don't want to be any trouble."

Daniel glanced in the rearview mirror, and Adaline saw the way his expression softened as it always did when he looked at Will. "No trouble at all, buddy. My mom's been planning it all week. I think she's more excited than you are."

"Impossible! I've been counting down the days since Monday," Will told him. "Only two more sleeps!"

Daniel glanced over at Adaline and when she turned to meet his gaze, he looked away. It didn't seem like he was mad at her, just wounded.

"That's a great kid you have," Daniel said, talking to Adaline.

"Do you wish you had kids too?" Will asked.

Adaline's breath caught and she waited for Daniel to answer.

"Yeah, I guess so." Daniel looked into the rearview to smile back at Will. "Especially if any kid of mine was as great as you."

Adaline felt the pull in her spirit. She needed to tell him. What was she waiting for?

"What about a wife? Most men your age have wives," Will commented, sounding older than his almost-nine years.

"All in God's timing, buddy," Daniel told him.

"That's exactly what my mom says," Will said. "She's waiting for Mr. Right."

Adaline covered her face with one hand.

Daniel reached over and touched her arm, the warmth of his skin reaching her heart. "Your mom already has Mr. Right," he said.

Will gave an audible "huh?" from the back seat.

"She has you, buddy." Daniel flicked his gaze to the mirror. Then he removed his hand from Adaline's arm and placed it back on the steering wheel.

As Daniel parked his truck near the baseball diamond and prepared to get out, Adaline reached for his arm, her fingers wrapping around his forearm before she could second-guess herself. "Daniel…"

He looked at her with concern. "What's wrong?"

It was time, but the timing wasn't at this moment. Not with Will in the back seat, but she always had Will with her.

"I want to talk to you," she said, her voice barely above a whisper. "Alone."

"Okay." Daniel's gaze searched hers. "Now?"

"No." She shook her head. "Right now, you two have practice," she said, stating the obvious.

Daniel glanced toward the field where other players were already warming up. "We sure do. There's a Little League game to prepare for."

Will cheered from the back seat.

Adaline nodded, reluctantly releasing his arm. "But soon, okay?"

"How about tomorrow night, Friday evening?" Daniel suggested. "We could go to dinner, maybe that new place in Millerville?"

Adaline had considered going to the Single Mothers Support Group at church, but this was more important. Lately, telling Daniel the truth was all she could think about. She couldn't wait any longer. "Tomorrow night," she agreed.

"Can I come too?" Will piped up from the back seat. "I love going to restaurants!"

Daniel turned to face Will. "Sorry, sport. It's just your mom and me tomorrow night. How are we supposed to pick out some special birthday surprises for your party this weekend if you're with us?"

Will bounced in the back seat. "You're going to get me surprises?"

"Maybe. But only if you promise not to peek when we bring them to the farm on Saturday."

"I promise! I won't even look in your direction when you're carrying them!"

Daniel helped Will out of the truck and stabilized him with his walker before walking toward the dugout.

Adaline wanted to go with Will, but that would have mortified him and Will was in good hands with Daniel. Instead, she took her usual place on the bleachers. The evening air was warm and filled with the sounds of children laughing and parents calling out encouragement. She watched Daniel with the team, marveling at his natural ability to include every child, especially Will.

Because of Daniel, Will was not just participating in the sport; with Daniel's modifications, he was thriving. Daniel was an amazing coach, and he would be an amazing father as well. Just the thought of coming clean with him had Adaline picking at her nailbeds as she tried to focus on the practice. Her mind continually wandered and played out various scenarios for when she told Daniel that he was a father.

"If I had to guess from your expression, you're not a fan of baseball."

Adaline looked up as Mrs. Matthews settled onto the bleacher beside her.

"Mrs. Matthews. I didn't expect to see you here tonight."

"I wanted to watch my son in action with the little ones," Mrs. Matthews explained with a warm smile. Then she turned to face Adaline directly, something serious in her eyes. "I also wanted to watch my grandson in action."

For a moment, Adaline was confused. Then her deeply furrowed brow smoothed out as understanding dawned.

Mrs. Matthews patted Adaline's thigh, nodding as if Adaline's stunned silence had confirmed everything she needed to know. She looked back out on the field where Will was currently at the batting tee with Daniel crouched beside him, adjusting his stance.

Adaline's heart pounded so hard that she was certain Mrs.

Matthews could hear it. She tried to speak, but her throat felt completely closed.

"The question is," Mrs. Matthews continued gently, "do you plan to tell Daniel?"

"I..." Adaline struggled to find her voice. "I'm going to tell him tomorrow night at dinner."

Mrs. Matthews smiled just enough. "Good. That's good."

"Mrs. Matthews, I—" How could Adaline possibly explain nine years of silence? How could she justify keeping a father from his son? A grandmother from her grandson?

Mrs. Matthews reached over and squeezed Adaline's hand. "I've always loved you like a daughter, Adaline. You know that. But I need to warn you that Daniel is going to be heartbroken that he didn't know he had a son all this time. And rightfully so."

Tears stung Adaline's eyes. "Are you heartbroken too? That you didn't know you had a grandson?"

Mrs. Matthews laughed, a sound so warm and genuine that it took Adaline by surprise. "Oh, sweetheart. I suspected the truth all along. Why do you think I've been asking you and Will over for dinner so often?"

It was true. Mrs. Matthews invited Adaline and Will over to their house at least once a month. Adaline just assumed Mrs. Matthews was being nice but maybe there was more to it.

"Why do you think I was so insistent about Daniel driving you to school and about having Will's birthday party at our farm?" Mrs. Matthews asked.

Adaline lowered her head. "You never said anything."

"It was just a suspicion. I didn't know for sure until that first Sunday that Daniel was back at church. Seeing him and Will side by side... Your boy has Daniel's eyes, you know. And his smile. He even tilts his head when he's thinking hard about something the same way my son does. He's the spitting image of Daniel." Mrs. Matthews's voice grew soft. "I've just been waiting for God's timing to bring Daniel home and for confirmation on my suspicions. God's timing is always best."

Out on the field, Will successfully made contact with the ball on the tee. He tapped the arm of his peer runner, sending the child racing toward first base. The other teammates cheered wildly. Daniel shouted encouragement too, looking like a child himself.

"He's going to be a wonderful father," Mrs. Matthews said quietly. "He already is, even if he doesn't know it yet."

Adaline agreed as she watched, her heart breaking and healing simultaneously. "Mrs. Matthews?" she said softly.

"Yes, dear?"

"Thank you. For not judging me."

Mrs. Matthews squeezed her hand. "That's what mothers do, Adaline. We love our children no matter what. And you, my dear, have always been one of mine."

Tears burned Adaline's eyes. She'd never had a mother figure in her life. It meant the world to her that Mrs. Matthews thought of her that way. The weight on Adaline's shoulders slowly eased. Would Daniel be as forgiving tomorrow night? Would his feelings for her change?

The kids all cheered when Will's peer runner rounded third into home. Mrs. Matthews patted Adaline's hand again. "He'll need time, but he'll come around the bases."

Daniel paused as he walked up on Will sitting alone on the dugout bench after practice. The boy's shoulders were slumped and Daniel didn't think it was because he was tired. Where was Adaline?

Daniel looked around, noting that the parking lot was emptying as parents gathered their children and equipment.

"Hey, sport." He settled on the bench beside Will. "You

played great in that mock game tonight. That hit in the fourth inning was perfect."

Will looked up, offering a weak smile that didn't quite reach his eyes. "Thanks, Coach Daniel, but nothing's perfect. Except Jesus. That's what Pastor Matthews always says."

The irony wasn't lost on Daniel. "My dad said that to me a lot when I was growing up. He still says it."

Will seemed to assess whether Daniel was joking or being serious. "I'm not sad about losing the mock game."

"Oh." Daniel scratched the side of his cheek, searching for another reason that Will might look so defeated. "What's on your mind then? You look like you're carrying the weight of the world on those shoulders of yours."

"I try not to compare myself to the other kids," Will finally said, "but sometimes I wonder why God gave me cerebral palsy. Why do I have to be different?"

A knot of unexpected emotion tightened Daniel's throat. He remembered asking similar questions at Will's age, though for different reasons. The weight of being the pastor's son and the expectations that came with that role set him apart from his peers in ways that sometimes felt more like a burden than a blessing. "I'd like to say I know how you feel, but I don't." He shook his head. "I've always been the fastest runner and I had the highest batting average."

Will frowned. "You're not helping, Coach Daniel."

"I'm trying. When I was your age, I felt like I had to be the best because being Pastor Matthews's son put me under a microscope." Daniel leaned in, eager to use some fragment of his life to comfort Will. This was what he wanted to do with the youth group teens too. "I felt like I had to get good grades and be on my best behavior. I had to do everything just right. The pressure, well, it made me feel like I couldn't breathe sometimes."

Will's eyebrows slowly rose, curiosity replacing some of his sadness.

"I used to pray and ask God why He had to give me a dad who was the town's only pastor. Why couldn't I just have a normal dad?"

"I like Pastor Matthews," Will offered.

"Me too, sport. He's my dad. I love him. My point is, we all feel different sometimes. We all wonder why God made us the way He did and put us where we are. But you know what I learned?"

Will's lips slightly parted. "What?"

"God doesn't make mistakes. He wasn't trying to make your life harder when He gave you cerebral palsy. I suspect He knew you were strong enough to handle it. And look at what you're doing. You're playing baseball and making new friends. You're showing everyone around you what determination looks like." Daniel studied Will's face. "You inspire people, Will. You inspire me."

A genuine smile spread across Will's features. "I do?"

"I think you're one of the bravest kids I know. In fact, I know you are."

Will launched himself into Daniel's chest and Daniel's arms instinctively tightened around him for a hug. Holding this boy felt so natural. So right. Will was a great kid and Daniel suspected that he would do great things for God. Daniel wanted to be here to watch that happen.

"Will?" Adaline's voice called from behind them.

They both looked up to see her standing a few feet away, watching them with an unreadable expression. Daniel wondered how long she'd been there and what she'd heard. He remembered that she'd wanted to tell him something earlier, and they'd agreed to talk tomorrow night over dinner.

It wasn't a date, even though he wouldn't mind if it were.

She'd already told him she couldn't forget how he'd broken her heart though. How could they start over when the sins of his past were always at the forefront of her mind?

"Where have you been?" Adaline asked Will. "I saw all of the other kids heading off field and I assumed you'd be with them. I waited outside the bathroom area for you."

"I've been here the whole time," Will said. "I'm kind of tired."

"Oh." She looked at Daniel and back at Will. "Well, that makes sense. You played hard. It was a great game."

"It was just a mock game. But my side still lost," Will said with a tiny frown.

Daniel ruffled Will's hair affectionately. "I guess no one ever told you the secret about baseball."

Will and Adaline both looked at him.

"Losers still win because they get ice cream afterward," Daniel said, whispering to Will loud enough for Adaline to hear too. "Even for mock games."

Will's eyes lit up like Christmas morning, and he looked at his mother hopefully. "Can we, Mom? Please?"

Daniel watched Adaline's expression shift from worry to humor to hesitation. Then she sighed and looked at Will with such pure, unconditional love. She was beautiful inside and out. Caring, nurturing, and God-loving too. How had he fumbled his perfect partner so completely?

He realized that tomorrow was a school day, so he quickly offered, "We could do drive-through ice cream. Nothing too crazy." Her smile made Daniel's heart skip a beat.

"Okay. Ice cream sounds good."

Will's cheer echoed through the dugout.

"Too tired to walk?" Daniel asked. "Because I can put you on my shoulders."

Will's grin was contagious. "That's okay. I suddenly don't

feel so tired anymore." He grabbed hold of his walker and stood.

"Parents get ice cream too, you know," Daniel told Adaline as he helped Will steady himself on the sidewalk.

"Coach Daniel, you're not a parent," Will piped up. Then, with the innocent curiosity that only children possessed, he asked, "Do coaches get ice cream?"

Daniel laughed. "Coaches get two scoops, buddy."

An hour later, after a trip to the local ice cream shop, Daniel pulled into Adaline's driveway with Will fast asleep in the back seat of his truck, a smile stamped on his face.

"I'll carry him in," Daniel offered quietly, getting out of the truck.

Adaline started to protest, but Daniel was already carefully lifting Will from the back seat, marveling at how light the boy felt in his arms. Will stirred slightly but didn't wake as Daniel carried him up the front steps and into the house.

Adaline led him to Will's room, and Daniel gently placed the boy on his Lightning McQueen–themed comforter. As Adaline quietly helped Will out of his cleats and baseball uniform, Daniel looked around the room. There were drawings on the walls, school awards, baseball cards and family photos, but notably, he didn't see any pictures of Will's father. Maybe Will was too young to remember him. Or the memories were too painful.

As they stepped back into the hallway and walked into the living room, Daniel lingered. "What time should I pick you up tomorrow night? For dinner?"

Adaline's relaxed expression tensed.

"Whatever you want to tell me, it'll be okay, Addie. If you want to tell me that you can't forgive me after all, I'll accept it. I won't like it, but I'll do what you need me to."

"That's not what I want to discuss," she said quietly.

Relief poured over him. "Okay, well, whatever it is, it won't change the fact that you're the one who got away for me. I could never think any more or less of you." He offered his pinkie finger, feeling slightly ridiculous but hoping she'd remember their old tradition. At first, she stared at him like he'd lost his mind, but then recognition dawned in her eyes. When they were teenagers, a pinkie promise had been all they'd ever needed because they'd trusted each other completely.

Of course, he'd broken that trust when he broke her heart. Maybe she needed more than a pinkie promise these days to believe him.

Surprising him, Adaline lifted her hand and curled her little finger around his. "You can pick me up tomorrow night at six."

# *Chapter Nine*

"The…cat…sat…on…the…" Adaline's third-grade student, Marcus, paused and squinted at the next word. "Ms. Harper, I don't know this one."

"Take your time," Adaline encouraged gently. "What do you see at the beginning of the word?"

"*M*," Marcus said with certainty.

"That's right. And what sound does *m* make?"

Marcus seemed to think for a moment and then his body straightened and he said, "Mmm," excitedly.

"Excellent! Now look at the rest of the letters. What do you think the word might be?"

Marcus stared at the page for another long moment before his face brightened. "Mat! The cat sat on the mat!"

This was the equivalent of a home run in Adaline's world. "See? You just needed to take your time with it."

Marcus slumped back in his chair, the brief moment of success already fading. "This is so hard, Ms. Harper. I'm never going to be good at reading. All the other kids are way better than me."

Adaline's heart held a familiar ache. She'd seen this discouragement in so many students over the years, and in her own son. They compared themselves to their peers and found themselves lacking.

"Reading takes practice and patience, Marcus. Even the

best readers in your class had to learn these same skills when they were younger."

"I don't have patience," Marcus said matter-of-factly. "That's what my parents always say about me."

Adaline felt a familiar pang of concern. "Well, patience is also a skill that can be worked on, just like reading."

Marcus looked up at her. "My grandmother told me that I can pray when I need help." He shrugged. "So I'll just ask God to give me patience."

Adaline smiled. "I think that's an excellent strategy, Marcus," she said.

"My mom told me once that if you pray for patience, God will put things in your life that are hard," Marcus said. "She said she prayed for patience one time, and then she found out she was pregnant with me."

Adaline kept her expression neutral, but inside, her heart broke a little for this boy. She knew his mother was likely joking, but jokes like that slowly chipped away at a child's sense of worth and belonging. Adaline remembered the feeling well from her own childhood, growing up with a dad who was more concerned with his own convenience than with nurturing his daughter's heart.

"Marcus," Adaline said carefully, "sometimes grown-ups say things they don't really mean, especially when they're tired or stressed. But I want you to know that children are gifts from God. You are a gift. Your mom and dad love you very much, even when things feel hard."

Uncertainty lingered in his young eyes. She wanted to say more, but she knew it would only be words. Kids needed action. They needed the adults in their life to show them how to live and succeed. Adaline hadn't had an adult like that in her life, but fortunately Mrs. Matthews had filled in the voids in her young adulthood, teaching her what it meant to be a good parent for Will.

The bell rang, signaling the end of the school day, and Marcus gathered his backpack and papers. "I'll see you at Will's birthday party this weekend, Ms. Harper!"

Adaline hadn't realized Marcus was on the invite list. "You're coming to Will's party?"

"Yep! Will invited almost everyone in the whole school. He said there's going to be horses and a barn and everything!" Marcus waved as he headed toward the door where children were spilling into the halls. "Thanks for helping me with reading today!"

"You're welcome," she called back as he disappeared out of sight.

Will had invited the entire school? When she'd mentioned the growing guest list to Mrs. Matthews, the older woman had simply said that the more children that came, the merrier. Adaline doubted Mrs. Matthews meant all of Prairie Elementary School's students though.

A ding from her cell phone interrupted her thoughts. Hurrying over to her desk, she tapped the screen and saw a text from Daniel.

Your car is fixed! I parked it in the school lot so you and Will can drive home in your own vehicle today. Keys are under the front mat. —D

"Yes!" she said out loud. Having her own transportation meant independence and normalcy. It also meant the ability to come and go without depending on Daniel's schedule. Another text came through immediately.

I'll still pick you up at 6 for dinner tonight though. Looking forward to it.

Adaline's stomach fluttered with a mixture of anticipation and dread. Everything was about to change, but she wasn't sure if it would be for the better or for the worse.

"Mom?" Will turned the corner, entering her classroom with his walker clicking against the linoleum floor. He paused to look at her. "Why do you look so happy?"

Adaline tilted her head to one side, giving him a curious look. When had joy become so rare in their daily life that Will noticed it as an anomaly? "I'm happy because you're here and I've missed you all day." Adaline slipped her phone into her pocket and walked over to where Will was standing.

"If you missed me so much, then can I come to dinner with you and Coach Daniel tonight?" he asked.

Adaline laughed. "Nice try, sweetheart, but no. This is grown-up-talk time."

Will looked skeptical. "You can have grown-up talk on the way home today."

"Good news," Adaline told him. "Our car is fixed. We can drive ourselves home."

Instead of excitement, Will's eyes grew glassy. "But I wanted to tell Coach Daniel about my day. And I wanted to ask him if he thinks my batting stance is getting better."

The longing in Will's voice made it clear just how much he needed a father figure in his life. Daniel's presence over the past weeks had filled a void she hadn't fully recognized before because acknowledging it meant admitting what she'd robbed both Will and Daniel of all these years.

After tonight, the truth would be out in the open. Daniel might be angry, hurt or confused. He might want nothing to do with her afterward. Worst case, he wouldn't want anything to do with either of them. She couldn't imagine Daniel taking his feelings out on Will though. In fact, she trusted that Daniel's bond with Will wouldn't change.

Trust. She trusted Daniel again. Now, she needed to gain back his trust.

She looked at Will, memorizing his hopeful expression. Not just Daniel's trust. She'd have to earn back Will's trust too. She hated that she'd let him down, but she wouldn't compare herself to her own parents. Her mother had never tried to make amends and her father never thought he'd done anything wrong. The fact that Adaline knew she'd messed up and was taking steps to make things right…well, that was the kind of progress her students made daily. Small. Incremental. But moving in the right direction.

"Will," she said softly as she grabbed her teacher bag, "Mrs. Beth is bringing Carson over to hang out with you tonight. You're going to watch a movie and eat pizza for dinner."

Will bounced happily. "Really?"

"Yep. They won't arrive for a couple hours though. How about we go home and you can call Coach Daniel before dinner? You can tell him all about your day over the phone. Would that work?"

Will's smile widened. "Can I tell him about the reading group and the math test that I aced?"

He hadn't even told her those things. A new fear unlocked. What if Daniel did become the person her son turned to and told things to? He'd always been a momma's boy because Adaline was all Will had. Would he soon be a daddy's boy? Was she about to lose more than she realized?

"Of course, you can, sweetheart."

Will cheered, pushing his walker faster. "Great. I can't wait to call Coach. Let's go, Mom!"

* * *

Daniel rubbed his sweaty palms on his navy pants before walking up to Adaline's front door. Like his mother preparing for church on a Sunday morning, he'd changed clothes three times, finally settling on a button-down shirt and dress pants. He wanted to look like this outing with Adaline meant something to him because it did. Now he wondered if he was too dressed up. Did he look like he was trying too hard?

When Adaline opened the door, Daniel prepared to say hello, but his mind couldn't connect with his mouth as she smiled back at him, wearing a simple blue dress coupled with a lightweight cardigan. Her light brown hair was set in soft waves tonight, hanging loosely on her shoulders. For a moment, he was that seventeen-year-old guy, more than a boy, but not quite a man, picking her up for their first real date. He remembered the feeling. It had been terrifying in a good way.

"You look, um, well..." He stopped and started, trying to figure out what was appropriate right now. This wasn't a date and he had no idea what she wanted to discuss.

"You polish up nicely, Coach," Adaline told him.

"Thanks. So do you." He flinched. "Not that you needed to polish up. You're always beautiful, Addie."

Her cheeks blushed. Maybe calling her beautiful was a little too much for a nondate.

"Ready to go?" he asked.

"I am. I'll just grab my bag and meet you at the truck." She disappeared behind her front door, leaving Daniel to wonder if he should wait on the porch steps. Instead, he headed back down the driveway and opened the passenger side door of his truck.

When she reappeared, she smiled as she approached. "Always the gentleman," she teased.

"My dad taught me well." He closed the door behind her

once her feet were tucked under the dash. She deserved a gentleman. Adaline deserved so much more than he had given her more than a decade ago.

As they drove through the familiar streets of Prairie, in his peripheral vision he saw Adaline glancing over at him. "So where are we going again? You mentioned a new restaurant?"

"I changed my mind," Daniel said. "I thought maybe we could go to our favorite restaurant." He caught Adaline's confused expression before returning his gaze to the road. "Don't tell me you've forgotten our place?"

"We had a place?" Adaline asked, making Daniel chuckle.

"Mrs. Corbin's place on the water. Remember? I used to take you there when we were dating. She always insisted we eat for free because she attended Dad's church and said she wanted to give back to Pastor Matthews's family."

"Ah, yes, that's right. Is she still giving you free meals?"

"No." Daniel shook his head slightly. "I mean, she would probably want to, but I'm paying." From his peripheral, he saw Adaline tense.

"Oh, I can't ask you to pay. This isn't a date and you don't even…"

"Have a job?" he asked, finishing her thought.

She tugged her lower lip between her teeth. "I didn't say that. I almost did, but I know you work hard helping your parents on the farm. And you're coaching Little League. You have plenty of jobs. I just… Well, you've already done so much for me. I tried to pay Andrew Neally for repairing my car and he said the bill was covered. Daniel, you really didn't have to do that," she said, talking fast.

Daniel sensed that this had been weighing heavy on her mind. "You always did have a hard time accepting a gift."

"Paying for my car was more than a gift. It kind of felt like charity," she said quietly.

"Adaline Harper is the last person who needs a handout. I know that," Daniel told her. "I just wanted to do something nice for you. You deserve kindness and generosity." She deserved every good thing that life had to offer. "I had lunch with Pastor Jason the other day and he paid for my meal. I figure that paying for yours would be kind of like paying it forward."

This made her smile, her shoulders relaxing at her sides. "If you insist."

"I do."

When they pulled into the restaurant's gravel parking lot, Daniel felt a wave of nostalgia wash over him. The weathered wooden building looked exactly the same, with its wraparound porch overlooking the lake and string lights that would soon twinkle in the gathering dusk.

Mrs. Corbin spotted them the moment they walked through the door. She was older now, her hair completely gray instead of the salt-and-pepper he remembered, but her smile was the same as she hurried over to engulf Daniel in a warm hug.

"Daniel Matthews! I was wondering when I'd see you in my restaurant again." She squeezed him tightly before stepping back to look him over. "And Adaline! Oh, honey, you look just as lovely as ever."

As Mrs. Corbin led them to a table by the window, she chattered excitedly about how good it was to see them together again. "I always wondered what happened to you two. I mean, I heard that you broke up, but I always hoped you'd find your way back to one another," she said, looking between them.

"Oh, we're not…" Adaline shook her head, her gaze meeting Daniel's as if expecting him to clear up the misunderstanding. There was no time to do so though because Mrs.

Corbin continued talking as she settled them at their table and leaned in conspiratorially.

"So tell me, Daniel, how's that fancy career treating you up in Atlanta? I heard you became quite the successful businessman."

Daniel felt the familiar urge to spin his usual tale of success and accomplishment, but he took a breath and reminded himself that true success wasn't about job titles or one's bank account. It was about the way he'd cheered Will up the other night at practice. The way he'd helped Adaline with her car.

"Actually, my career never really took off the way I hoped it would. I've been struggling for years, trying to make something work that just wasn't meant to be."

"Oh, honey." Mrs. Corbin reached over to pat his shoulder. "Things don't always work out the way we plan, do they? But you know what? God's plans are always better than ours, even when we can't see it at the time."

They took the seats that Mrs. Corbin guided them to and ordered catfish and hush puppies that tasted exactly like he remembered. The nostalgia of the food added to the same feeling of an easy conversation peppered with laughter.

Daniel told Adaline stories about his disastrous attempts at corporate life, and she shared updates about her work at the school and Will's latest adventures. When he made a particularly self-deprecating joke about his failed business ventures, Adaline laughed until she nearly spit out a swallow of sweet tea, looking like the young girl she'd once been. He'd always loved her laugh. It was contagious. Even though the conversation was easy, there was a tension in the air between them that Daniel suspected was related to whatever Adaline wanted to tell him. He waited for her to initiate that important conversation, but it didn't come during the meal.

When the meal was over, Daniel leaned forward and asked, "Do you want to take a walk along the lake?"

She glanced out the window, her mood turning serious. "Yes."

The evening air was cool and peaceful around them as they strolled. The sun was setting, painting the water in shades of gold and pink.

"I didn't have this view in Atlanta," he told her. "Or if I did, I didn't notice. I was too busy trying to be someone." He pointed at a bench ahead of them.

Without a verbal question, she nodded and followed him to sit down.

As they sat side by side, Daniel clasped his hands together and looked at her. "So," he said gently, "what was it you wanted to tell me?"

Adaline seemed to shiver at the question, but he resisted putting his arm around her for warmth. It wasn't cool tonight. In fact, the weather was perfect. What could be causing her such obvious distress? It didn't make sense.

A thought suddenly occurred to him that he'd never considered. Adaline had gotten married so soon after he'd ended their relationship. What if she'd already been seeing her late husband behind Daniel's back before they'd even broken up? What if Adaline was about to confess to cheating on him all those years ago? What if she'd gotten pregnant with Will before Daniel had even left Prairie?

Daniel's chest felt tight. Adaline hadn't attended church back then. She'd come from a broken home and her values weren't the same as what he'd grown up with. He'd thought they were exclusive. He'd even told her he loved her, but she never said it back.

"Addie?" He reached over to take her hand, noticing the tremble through her palm. "Whatever you're about to tell me, I want you to know that I won't be upset. If it's something that happened in the past, I know we were both different people back then." He squeezed her hand gently. Looking into her eyes, he meant every word. "I'm just grateful to be here with you tonight."

Her skin was pale. Her lips trembled. She really didn't look well, he realized.

"You know, you don't even have to tell me anything if you don't want to, Addie. I'm okay with clearing the slate without even knowing what was on it," he told her, beginning to worry.

"No." She shook her head quickly, her eyes welling with tears. "We can't clear the slate because the past affects the present. And our future."

Our future?

"Daniel, you need to know this," she said with conviction, pressing her eyes closed. "I can't keep this secret from you any longer."

"Okay." Now Daniel felt himself tremble. "Addie, what's going on?"

# *Chapter Ten*

Adaline gulped in the cool air, pulling it into her lungs as she looked out over the water, gathering every ounce of courage she possessed. *God, please help me*, she prayed silently, hoping Daniel would somehow understand.

Daniel squeezed her hand, waiting wordlessly.

*I can do this.* Turning, she faced the man she'd never quite gotten over. How could she when she had a physical reminder in her son staring back at her every morning?

"Will isn't Christopher's son," she began in barely a whisper.

"I—I'm not sure I understand."

He would though, soon enough. Would he continue to hold her hand once he did?

"Daniel, I was already pregnant when I started dating Christopher. He knew the baby wasn't his, but he didn't care because he'd always liked me as more than friends. He'd been asking me out for years before I started dating you, but I wasn't interested in him that way. I liked Christopher, but my heart didn't race when he walked into a room. Not the way it did with you."

She dared a glance at Daniel, gauging his reaction.

He stared blankly, the tiniest divot between his brows.

"It wasn't the perfect life I'd imagined, but Christopher was a good man. He was a loving father to Will. Christopher attended every doctor's appointment and every physical therapy session. He loved Will as if he were his own." That was one of the qualities Adaline loved most about her late husband.

"Addie, I'm not sure I understand what you're telling me."

She pulled in a ragged breath. "When Christopher died, I was devastated. Not as much for me but for Will. It seemed so unfair. If Will couldn't have his biological father, why couldn't he at least have his stepfather?"

Daniel looked shell-shocked, his eyes wide and unfocused as he stared out over the water. But he didn't look angry. He didn't look sad either. The silence stretched on until Daniel finally spoke, his voice hollow with disbelief. "Of course he loved Will. Will is the greatest kid I've ever met. Any man worth his salt would be blessed to be that kid's father. Christopher was a blessed man."

Adaline's stomach churned with guilt. "Daniel."

He looked at her. "You're going to have to spell this out for me, Addie, because I'm having a hard time understanding. Are you telling me that Will is my son?"

The pain in his eyes broke her. "Daniel, I know there's no good excuse for keeping this from you. I was heartbroken when you left, and I—I felt so betrayed. You'd promised to come back for me, and then you just… I didn't know what to do. I was eighteen and pregnant. I was scared. When Christopher asked me out, it felt like an answer to my prayer. And when he discovered I was pregnant, he didn't hesitate. He offered to marry me and it seemed like the only option that made sense. He was there, Daniel, and you left. Just like my mom, you walked away. The thought of you doing that to my son…"

"Our son," Daniel corrected with a clipped tone. "To our son. You didn't even give me a chance."

"I know. But the truth is," she said, desperate for him to

understand, "I was just young and foolish, and I made a terrible decision that I've regretted every single day since."

Daniel pulled his hand from hers and ran his fingers through his hair. The gesture was so achingly reminiscent of the young man she'd fallen in love with in high school that it made her chest tight with longing.

"We could have figured it out together. Addie, I've missed everything. My son's first steps, his first words, his first day of school. He's turning nine. I missed years of his life, and I didn't even know he was mine." He swallowed, looking pained. "The thought occurred to me for a millisecond, but then I told myself you would never do that to me. No matter how mad you were or how many trust issues you had, I told myself that you were a good person. You'd never keep something like us having a child together secret."

Adaline reached for his hand again, but he dodged the move.

"I actually felt guilty for even considering the thought because you are good and noble. That's what I thought." He scoffed. "I'll drive you home," he said, standing. He took slow steps in the direction of his truck, not bothering to check if she was following him. When he got to his truck, he still walked around and opened the passenger door, but he didn't wait to close it behind her.

She wanted to explain more as they drove in silence, but what else could she say? Daniel was right. She'd betrayed him and there was no excuse that justified her actions.

When Daniel parked in her driveway, Adaline reached for the door handle but didn't move.

"I'm sorry," she whispered.

Daniel still didn't look at her. The tension in the air between them was thick. So much for his claim that she could tell him anything and he wouldn't be upset. Not that she blamed him, but it just proved that no one's word was solid. No one except God.

"Yeah, me too," he said quietly.

Pushing the truck door open, Adaline stepped out and walked toward her front door, some part of her hoping Daniel would call out and ask her to wait. Instead, she heard the sound of his engine retreating in the driveway then fading into the distance.

*God, Your word says that You know the plans You have for me. Plans to help and not harm me. Despite how much I've made a mess of things... I need your help now. Please.*

Daniel left Adaline's house and drove aimlessly through the empty streets of Prairie. He just wasn't ready to head back to his parents' house. Adaline's confession left him feeling shaken. He couldn't believe Adaline would betray him in such a way.

Instead of turning toward home, he found himself driving past the road for his parents' neighborhood and pulling into the parking lot for Prairie Community Church. He'd expected the building to be empty this time of night, and that's what he needed. He wanted a quiet sanctuary where he could process this news. But as Daniel approached the front doors, he noticed light spilling from the windows of the sanctuary. His heart sank slightly and he considered turning back. Instead, he pushed through the doors, needing to be in this sacred space where he'd grown up.

Jason was sitting on the front pew as Daniel headed up the middle aisle. He turned to look over his shoulder. As Daniel drew closer, he saw sermon notes spread across Jason's lap and a worn Bible open beside him.

"Hey, Daniel. Everything okay?" Jason set his papers

aside, stacking them and making room on the pew for Daniel to sit if he wanted to.

"Sorry. I—I didn't really expect anyone to be here tonight." Daniel didn't move. "You're working. I should leave."

"No, man. I need a break anyway. The truth is, I usually work on this stuff from home, but something told me, probably God, that I needed to be here this evening." He looked at Daniel. "Maybe you're the reason." Jason gestured to the empty space beside him. "Want to talk about what's bothering you?"

"No," Daniel said automatically, but his feet carried him the rest of the way down the aisle anyway. "It's complicated."

"I may not have answers, but I can listen."

Daniel lowered himself to the pew, sitting a couple feet away from Jason. He released a long sigh and clasped his hands in front of him. "She told me Will is my son."

Jason went very still. "Adaline told you that?" he asked.

Daniel nodded. "Tonight. At dinner. Will isn't Christopher's son. He's, uh, he's mine. He's been my son all along."

The dam that Daniel had been holding back since leaving Adaline's house suddenly burst. His father had always taught him that it was okay for a man to cry and that tears were not a sign of weakness but still, Daniel rarely cried in front of others. He preferred to wrestle with his feelings in private. Here in God's house though, with Jason's steadying, nonjudgmental presence beside him, the tears rolled down his cheeks.

"I should be happy," Daniel said through his tears. "But I'm so ashamed by the way I turned from God, and of all the mistakes I made." He swallowed hard. "My hurt and anger turned into rebellion. I was the kid who helped my friends navigate their challenges, and the first one I faced, I completely turned my back on God. I know God has forgiven me."

"Of course he has," Jason agreed. "You're His prodigal son, Daniel."

Daniel looked at Jason, trying to make sense of his thoughts. "I guess, well, I guess I'm just trying to forgive myself fully. Will is my son. He's a blessing that God brought out of my sin."

"God is good." Jason laid a hand on Daniel's arm. "God can turn our sin into a testimony. If we surrender it to Him. Daniel, you think you've worked on this area of your life, but it's remained a secret that you've been running from. Adaline too."

Daniel wiped his eyes with the back of his hand. "Changing my career path wasn't just about wanting to step out of my father's shadow. I left Prairie and all the plans I'd made. I turned my back on everything, failing God, my family and the church. I never stopping believing in God. I was just angry and hurting."

Jason listened quietly, then spoke with gentle wisdom. "What the enemy meant for evil, God used for good. When you thought you weren't worthy of God's love, God gave you an amazing gift."

"A gift that Adaline kept hidden from me."

Jason blew out a breath. "I can see how it'd be easy to resent Adaline for not telling you. I mean, you came home often enough. She had lots of opportunity, right?"

Daniel furrowed his brow. He'd come home for holidays, but he usually didn't go to church at Prairie Community Church when he was here.

"You checked in on Adaline, probably called to see how she was."

Daniel shook his head before realizing that Jason was being sarcastic. "She got married soon after we broke up."

"Yeah." Jason nodded. "I went to her late husband's funeral. Adaline's a widow, you know? I'm sure you reached out to at least offer condolences."

Daniel hadn't done that. He hadn't reached out to Adaline at all. "I understand your point, but I don't need a load of guilt piled on top of all the other." Daniel loved Jason, but this version of tough love wasn't the kind of counseling Daniel needed right now. At least that's what he thought.

"Maybe not, but you do need a reality check," Jason said simply. "Take the past out of the equation and look at the bigger picture. Will is an amazing kid who has inspired our entire community. Despite his disability, he's overcome obstacles that would defeat most adults. He's been an incredible witness for God's strength and grace. You think God didn't know any of this would happen? Do you really think He was surprised when you stepped out of line? God is so good, so gracious and merciful, that He used your failure for His glory. Wow." Jason laughed. "Wow. It never fails to amaze me just how great our God is."

The truth of Jason's words hit Daniel like a physical blow. All these years, he'd been carrying guilt and shame, believing that his sin had disqualified him from God's service. But Will was living proof that God could redeem even the most complicated circumstances.

"How do I get past the anger I feel toward Adaline? I know forgiveness is what Christ calls us to, but I'll be honest, it's not easy."

Jason didn't miss a beat. "Jesus knows a lot about forgiving those who hurt Him too. You two should chat."

Daniel smiled, despite his mood.

"Forgiveness isn't a feeling, Daniel. It's a choice. And sometimes we have to make that choice over and over again until our hearts catch up with our will. I'm not saying it'll be easy, but I know your heart. I also know that Adaline is probably still in it."

"I couldn't take my eyes off Adaline all night. Not because she's beautiful, but because I admired her. She's done so much in the past decade. She's familiar but also an entirely new person. The same Adaline that I fell in love with except God has changed her."

Jason waited for Daniel to grow quiet. "Tomorrow is Will's birthday party," he said. "You're not just his coach anymore—you're his father. That changes everything."

Daniel felt a new wave of panic wash over him. "I don't know the first thing about being a father. What if I mess this up too?"

Jason patted his back reassuringly. "I've watched you with Will. You already love him like a father should. Love is most important. The rest will come."

Standing to leave, Jason gathered his materials and looked back at Daniel. "Stay as long as you need to, buddy. But I recommend you go home and get some sleep soon. Sometimes things feel clearer in the morning after a good night's rest."

Alone in the sanctuary, Daniel walked slowly to the altar and dropped to his knees in prayer. The familiar space wrapped around him like a comforting embrace.

"Father," he whispered, "I don't know how to feel right now. I'm grateful and humbled. But I'm also struggling with unforgiveness toward Adaline. And something else. Lord, I don't think she ever left my heart. How do I move forward loving her and also feeling such betrayal?"

Ephesians 4:32 came to mind, falling into the forefront like an answer to his impossible question: *And be ye kind one to another, tenderhearted, forgiving one another, even as God for Christ's sake hath forgiven you.*

In his heart, he knew what he had to do, but he had no idea

how. There was no step-by-step outline to pluck the seeds of unforgiveness out of his spirit.

Another thought unfolded in his mind. It wasn't a Bible verse, but it felt like truth. He opened his eyes and remembered where he was. The altar. In his youth, this was where he came and knelt. Where he left his burdens. Back then, he didn't think about how to fix any issues in his life; he simply surrendered them to God. And that's what he needed to do now. Leave the betrayal, the resentment, the anger and the hurt. Leave it here at the altar.

# Chapter Eleven

"So, how was your dinner?" Beth asked as soon as Adaline walked through her front door. Beth was one of the few who babysat Will because of Will's longtime friendship with her son, Carson.

An expectant smile curled Beth's lips as she waited, eyebrows high on her forehead. "Will was so excited tonight. I could barely get him to sleep, but I finally did," she said, raising a pointer finger. "Be prepared for him to ask you all the questions when he wakes up." She laughed softly and then broke into a yawn. "So, did you have a good time with Daniel?"

"Yes. The evening was fine." Adaline placed her purse on the coffee table. She broke into a yawn as well, hoping Beth would take the hint. "I hope Will lets me sleep in a little because I am so tired," she added for good measure.

"Tired?" Beth asked, concern tightening her features. "Good dates usually make it impossible to fall asleep. When I was dating my husband, I always found myself reliving every moment."

"It wasn't really a date," Adaline told her friend, not for the first time. "Thank you again for watching Will for me."

"I barely did anything. Carson and Will played all night. They tuckered one another out. We're looking forward to his party tomorrow. Will is so excited about the farm that he didn't stop talking except to breathe and eat a bowl of ice cream." She stood and began to stir Carson awake from where he was lying on the couch. "Get some rest and if you need help setting up tomorrow, call me. You know I don't mind."

"Thanks."

Adaline watched Beth get Carson to his feet, helping him along as he seemed to sleepwalk out the front door toward their car.

After Beth had left, Adaline locked the door and leaned against it, finally allowing her carefully maintained composure to crumble. The house felt too quiet, too empty, filled with the echoes of what had transpired just hours earlier.

Tiptoeing down the hallway to Will's room, she pushed open the door just enough to peek inside. He was sleeping peacefully, his brown hair tousled against the pillow, one arm flung over a stuffed dinosaur. He looked so young and innocent, completely unaware that his world had shifted on its axis this evening while he played with his friend.

All she'd ever wanted was to provide him with the safe, stable, loving childhood that she'd never had. Had she failed him? By keeping his birth father's identity a secret and allowing him to grow up believing his stepfather was his biological parent? She'd thought she was doing the right thing for everyone involved by marrying Christopher. That was her solution though, not God's. In the process of trying to fix the mess she'd made, she'd robbed Will of growing up with his real dad—Daniel.

She made her way to her favorite corner of the living room, where a comfortable reading chair sat next to a small table that held her Bible and prayer journal. This was her quiet place, where she came to be still with God and seek His guidance when life felt overwhelming. It felt that way now.

Adaline sat and pulled her prayer journal to her lap. Writing had always been an outlet for her and a way to process her emotions. While she prayed throughout each day, usually in one long run-on conversation that never fully ended, sometimes she needed to write her prayers down and see them on paper.

As she flipped to the next blank page, the journal fell open to an entry from a couple weeks ago. Adaline's breath caught as she read her own words:

> God, I feel like there's distance between us lately, and I don't understand why. I'm reading my Bible, I'm praying, I'm serving at the church and school. Where can I serve You better? How can I draw closer to You? I feel like You're trying to tell me something, but I keep missing it.

Adaline understood now. The distance she'd been feeling wasn't because God had moved away from her; it was because she'd been running from His gentle but persistent nudging to tell Daniel the truth. It was done now though. She'd mustered the courage and she'd told him everything.

On an exhale, she picked up her pen and began to write:

> Father, I finally did what You've been asking me to do. I told Daniel the truth about Will, and I'm terrified. I feel sad and guilty and ashamed, but I know this is a necessary process to get me to a place where I can walk in Your perfect purpose for my life. Help me trust that You will work all things together for good, even when I can't see how. Help Daniel to forgive me. Help me to forgive myself.

After she closed her prayer journal, Adaline's eyes fell on the notebook that contained the story she'd been working on in her free time. Inspired by Will, it was a tale about a boy with disabilities who discovers that God made him special for a reason and that everyone is handcrafted by the Creator in exactly the way they're meant to be. She'd been hoping to finish the story and maybe submit it to a publisher one day, thinking it might encourage other children who faced similar challenges.

Out of all her past snippets of stories left unfinished, this one felt different somehow. It was personal. She wanted to finish it, needed to, but the words refused to come no matter how hard she tried.

There certainly wouldn't be any progress on her story tonight. How was she supposed to wrestle with fictional characters when her real life felt like it was falling apart all around her? All she wanted to do was go to bed and sleep away the worry. She had a sinking feeling, however, she'd spend the night tossing and turning. Tomorrow all of Will's family and friends would gather to celebrate the anniversary of the day he was born, including for the first time ever, Will's own father.

The truth was a gift that she could give her son, but she wasn't sure how Will would handle it. She hadn't just kept a secret from Daniel; she'd kept it from Will too. How could a nine-year-old boy possibly grasp something she didn't quite understand herself? *God, please guide me. Guide all of us moving forward.*

The next morning, Adaline woke to the sound of her bedroom door creaking open, followed by the familiar clicking rhythm of Will's walker against the hardwood floor. She glanced at the clock on her nightstand. Only 5:47 a.m.? It was far too early to wake on a normal Saturday morning. Her son had never been able to sleep in on his birthday.

"Mom! Mom, wake up! I'm nine today!" Will's face was glowing in the early-morning light that filtered through Adaline's curtains.

"Happy birthday, sweetheart." Adaline sat up in bed and opened her arms for a hug.

Will carefully maneuvered his walker to the side of her bed and leaned in for an embrace, his small body vibrating with barely contained energy. "Can we do something special this morning before my party?" he asked, pulling back to look at her with those hazel eyes that reminded her so much of Daniel.

"What did you have in mind? Pancakes with chocolate chips? A trip to the park?" Adaline ran through the list of Will's favorite activities in her mind, already planning how to fit them in before the afternoon party at the Matthewses' farm.

But Will's answer caught her completely off guard. "I want to go see Grandpa Bobby."

Adaline's smile faltered. Her father. She hadn't visited him at Meadowbrook Assisted Living in months, maybe four or five. The last time she'd gone, the visit had been strained and uncomfortable, filled with awkward silences and the weight of years of disappointment between them.

"Sweetheart, Grandpa Bobby isn't expecting us," Adaline said carefully. Not to mention her father probably didn't even remember that today was Will's birthday. "And we have so much to do before your party this afternoon."

"Please, Mom?" Will's expression was so hopeful to see his grandfather that Adaline felt her defenses crumbling. "It's my birthday, and I just really want to see him, Mom."

How could she say no to that? Despite her own complicated

feelings toward her father, Will had always maintained an inexplicable affection for the man who had been such a distant figure in Adaline's own childhood. Maybe children were simply better at loving unconditionally than adults were. Despite the few-and-far-between visits, her father always gave Will a wheat penny from his collection. It was their thing together and perhaps what sealed their bond. So simple.

"Okay," Adaline agreed, swallowing the anxiety that rose in her chest. "Let me get dressed, and we'll go visit Grandpa Bobby."

"Yay!"

An hour later, they pulled into the parking lot of Meadowbrook Assisted Living, a sprawling single-story building with cheerful yellow siding that seemed at odds with the loneliness Adaline always felt when she visited. Will was practically bouncing in his seat. She helped him out and steadied him behind his walker.

As they made their way through the familiar corridors, past the community room, where elderly residents sat watching morning television, past the nurses' station, where a young woman smiled and waved, Adaline felt the old heaviness settling over her. Growing up, she'd never had the close father-daughter relationship that other girls seemed to take for granted. Her father had always seemed to view her as an inconvenience, especially after her mother abandoned the family when she was still a toddler. He'd provided the basics such as food, shelter and clothing, but emotional connection had been absent from their home.

Was that why she'd kept Will from Daniel all these years? Had her own father's emotional absence shaped her belief that fathers were unreliable? No, her mother shaped the belief that parents as a whole were unreliable, and her father confirmed it. She didn't question that belief until she met Daniel and was invited into his home. Mr. and Mrs. Matthews showed Adaline that parents could be supportive. They could be relied on.

"Room 127, right?" Will asked, pushing forward, ahead of her as he checked the numbers on all the doors.

"That's right," Adaline told him, growing nervous. What if her father wasn't happy to see them? She didn't want anything to upset Will on his birthday today.

"This one!" Will eagerly knock on the door marked 127.

"Come in!" her father's gravelly voice called from inside the room.

Will struggled to maintain his balance and pulled the heavy door handle down. Hurrying to help, Adaline pressed the handle and the door swung open, revealing Robert Kinsley sitting in his wheelchair by the window. He was dressed in a flannel shirt and khaki pants, his gray hair neatly combed back. When he saw who his visitors were, his face lit up with delight.

"Grandpa Bobby!" Will said.

"Will! Adaline! What a wonderful surprise this is!" He wheeled himself toward them, his movements practiced despite the tremor in his hands from the Parkinson's disease that had necessitated his move to assisted living last year. "I was just thinking about you, you know," he told Will.

Will's eyes rounded. "You were? Really?"

His father's grin brought back memories from Adaline's childhood. Good memories. "Today's your birthday, correct?" He looked to Adaline for confirmation.

Adaline gave a slight nod, grateful for her father's memory. She was also shocked. He'd missed her birthday in January, and she'd shoved it off, chalking it up to his illness.

"You hungry?" her father asked. "Because I'm starving. I was just about to head down to breakfast." He gestured toward the door. "The cafeteria serves until nine. Care to join me?"

"Yes!" Will exclaimed immediately.

Adaline really didn't want to go eat in a crowded room full of people she didn't know, but the decision seemed to have been made. She was a little hungry, however.

"Are you too big to ride on my lap?" her father asked Will. "This power chair moves fast, you know."

Will giggled. "I'm nine years old, Grandpa Bobby," he said. "I'll use my walker."

Will led the two down the hall toward the cafeteria, which was bustling with residents. They found a table near the window, and Adaline helped her father navigate his wheelchair into position while Will settled beside him, his walker parked against the wall nearby. The conversation started with safe topics, such as Will's excitement about his birthday party, his progress in school and being on the Prairie Dogs Little League team.

As Adaline listened to Will chatter enthusiastically about Coach Daniel and baseball practice, she found herself observing her father's face. There was genuine interest there, etched between the deep wrinkles around his eyes and smile. She couldn't remember him ever showing interest with her hobbies at that age. Maybe he'd changed. Or maybe, like her, he was trying to do better with the second generation than he'd managed with the first.

"Adaline," her father said during a lull in Will's monologue about batting averages, "I've… Well, I've missed you."

The simple statement hung in the air between them, weighted with years of unspoken hurt and disappointment.

"I know I haven't been by in a while," Adaline said, feeling guilty. "Things have been busy with work and Will's therapy and—"

"That's not what I meant," her father interrupted gently. "I only meant that I've missed you for years. For most of your life, if I'm being honest." He looked down at his trembling hands, then back up at her with something like regret. "I want to apologize for not being a better dad when you were growing up. After your mother left, I just… I didn't know how to deal with anything, least of all a young daughter who needed so much more than I knew how to give."

Adaline hadn't realized how desperately she'd needed to hear those words until they were spoken aloud. Tears sprang to her eyes, years of hurt and longing suddenly rushing to the surface. She stood abruptly and moved around the table to embrace her father, feeling his frail shoulders beneath her arms, his body so much smaller than she remembered.

"I forgive you, Dad," she whispered, and meant it with every fiber of her being.

Will, seated next to his grandfather, seemed to understand the significance of the moment. He leaned over and wrapped his arms around both of them, creating a three-way hug that felt like healing.

When they finally pulled apart, Will reached down to where he'd placed his backpack beneath his chair. Adaline watched in surprise as he pulled out a wrapped, rectangular package. She hadn't realized he'd brought anything with him.

"This is for you, Grandpa Bobby." Will offered the gift with both hands.

Her father's eyes widened. "For me? But it's your birthday, son."

Will shrugged. "Giving gifts is fun too. And I wanted you to have this."

Adaline watched as her father carefully unwrapped the package, his hands shaking slightly as he tore away the paper. Inside was a leather-bound Bible, its cover pristine and unmarked. Adaline recognized it as one that Will had gotten from the church when he was baptized two years ago. He already had a Bible of his own, so he'd tucked it away on his shelf.

"Thank you," her father said, his voice thick with emotion as he pulled Will close again. "I needed one of these. I've been meaning to start reading the Bible." He clutched the Bible to his chest. "Thank you, Will."

"Maybe next time we come, we can bring the book my mom is writing," Will said brightly. "It's about a boy like me who learns that God made him special on purpose."

Adaline's cheeks burned. She hadn't talked much about her writing with her father. She hadn't thought he would be interested in that part of her life. But her father nodded, looking at her with something that might have been pride.

"I'd love to read it, Adaline. I'd be honored."

On the drive home, Will couldn't stop talking about the rest of the day's plans: the party at the farm, the horses he'd get to feed, the birthday cake Mrs. Matthews was making. But then he grew quiet for a moment, looking out the window at the passing houses.

"Mom, we should visit Grandpa Bobby more often," he said thoughtfully.

"You're right, sweetheart. We should."

Will was quiet for another moment before adding softly, "I wish I had a dad to hang out with too."

Adaline's hands tightened on the steering wheel, her heart clenching with the weight of the secret she'd been carrying. Will did have a father, and unknowingly, he would be hanging out with him and celebrating his birthday that very afternoon. Daniel would be there at the farm, helping to set up the party, coaching Will through games, probably carrying him on his shoulders at some point like he'd been doing at baseball practices.

The relationship between a father and child was so important. Even now, as an adult, she'd felt the healing power of her own father's apology, the restoration of a connection she'd thought was broken beyond repair. How much more important was it for Will to know his father while he was still young, while there was time to build memories and connections that would last a lifetime?

As they pulled into their driveway, Adaline sent up a silent prayer. Soon, Will would know who his father really was. And maybe, just maybe, God's grace would cover her mistakes the way it had covered the distance between her and her own father this morning.

Today was Will's ninth birthday. By his tenth, she promised herself, everything would be different. He would know the truth, and their family would finally be complete. Hopefully.

## *Chapter Twelve*

Daniel woke before dawn on Will's ninth birthday, his mind immediately flooding with the overwhelming reality that had kept him awake most of the night. He had a son. A nine-year-old son. And he'd missed every single birthday before this one.

He lay in bed staring at the ceiling of his childhood bedroom, listening to the familiar sounds of the farm awakening, his father's footsteps in the hallway and the distant crow of the rooster. Everything was the same as it had been for thirty years, except that Daniel's entire world had shifted on its axis.

Today was Will's birthday party at the farm. Aside from baseball, Will had been talking about nothing else in Daniel's presence. He was so excited, and so was Daniel except...he didn't have a gift for Will. What do you give a child you've just discovered is your son? What could possibly make up for eight previous birthdays missed, eight years of "Happy Birthday" songs unsung and eight cakes without candles blown out together?

By eight o'clock, Daniel was dressed and heading into town, his truck rumbling down the quiet streets of Prairie as the sun began to light up the sky in shades of pink and orange. Main Street was just beginning to wake up. The bakery had its lights on and old Mr. Henderson was sweeping the sidewalk in front of his hardware store as he had since Daniel was Will's age.

Daniel parked near the town square and began his search for the perfect gift. He tried the big box store in town first, wandering through aisles of action figures and board games, but nothing felt right. Will wasn't like other nine-year-olds. His cerebral palsy meant that many typical toys would be frustrating rather than fun. Daniel picked up and put down a dozen different items, each one feeling more inadequate than the last.

The bookstore was next. Daniel had recently learned that Will loved to read, but which books? What did nine-year-olds read these days? Daniel found himself staring at shelves of children's literature, overwhelmed by choices and frozen by the realization that he didn't know his own son well enough to make an informed decision.

How many other fathers knew their sons this poorly? How many had missed the crucial years of building blocks and bedtime stories, of scraped knees and first days of school? The weight of everything he'd lost pressed down on Daniel's chest until he could barely breathe.

Finally, almost by instinct, Daniel found himself at Prairie Sports & Recreation, the store where he'd bought his first baseball glove at Will's age. The familiar smell of leather drew him as he stepped inside.

Baseball. It was the one thing he and Will shared, the one place where they'd built a connection over the past few weeks. Maybe he couldn't give Will back the lost years, but he could give him something that represented their future together.

Daniel found himself in front of the display of youth baseball gloves, running his fingers over the smooth leather, testing the weight and flexibility of different models. He finally selected one that was the right size for Will's hands, with good padding and a deep pocket that would help compensate for any coordination challenges.

This was good, but it still didn't feel like enough. It was too simple, too impersonal. He needed to make it special somehow and mark this moment as significant.

Milo Jenson came to mind. His friend had been engraving on wood and leather for ages. Daniel pulled out his phone and dialed, glancing at his watch. It was still early, but Milo had a newborn baby at home. Daniel guessed that meant he was probably awake.

"Hello?" Milo's voice was tired and slightly harried, and in the background, Daniel could hear the unmistakable wail of a crying baby.

"Milo, it's Daniel. Sorry to call so early."

"No worries, man. We've been up since four. Little Emma decided she's not a fan of sleep." Milo chuckled despite his obvious exhaustion. "What's up?"

Daniel explained about the baseball glove and asked if Milo could engrave something on it on very short notice. "I know it's last minute, and with the baby—"

"I'll do it right now," Milo interrupted. "Seriously, Daniel, I owe you big time for taking over the Little League coaching this season. Sarah and I wouldn't have survived these first few weeks with Emma if I'd been trying to run practices too."

"You don't owe me anything," Daniel said, feeling humbled by Milo's gratitude. "Coaching that team has been a huge and unexpected blessing for me. More than you know."

And it was true. If he hadn't taken over coaching, he might never have gotten to know Will and might never have discovered the truth about his son. God's timing was mysterious and perfect.

"Well, whatever you say, I'm happy to help. Bring the mitt

over now, and it'll be ready before the party this afternoon," Milo said. "Don't mind the crying baby in the background."

The teasing tone in Milo's voice suggested he expected Daniel to make an excuse about the noise or the inconvenience. But Daniel surprised himself with his response.

"I'd love to hold her while you work," he said, the words coming from somewhere deep in his chest. He'd never gotten to hold Will when he was a baby. "I mean, if you don't mind."

There was a pause on the other end of the line. "Of course, man. Come on over. We'd be happy to have you."

"I'll be right there," Daniel said, already heading toward the checkout counter to pay for the glove.

Twenty minutes later, Daniel was sitting in Milo and Sarah's living room, cradling one-month-old Emma in his arms while Milo worked at his engraving station in the corner. The baby had stopped crying almost immediately when Daniel had picked her up, and now she stared up at him with unfocused blue eyes, her tiny fist wrapped around his finger with surprising strength.

She was so small and fragile. Had Will been this small once? Had he fit in the crook of Adaline's arm this way, his whole body lighter than a sack of flour? Daniel tried to imagine Adaline at nineteen, alone and scared to tell him that he was the father, facing all the physical challenges of Will's cerebral palsy.

The ache in his chest intensified, but it was mixed with something else now. Not just regret for what he'd lost, but gratitude for what he still had the chance to gain. He might have missed Will's infancy and toddlerhood, his first words and first steps. But God had given him back his son, and there were still so many moments ahead to be part of.

"What do you want me to engrave?" Milo asked, holding up the glove.

Daniel thought for a moment, still rocking Emma gently.

"Colossians 3:23," he said finally. "'And whatsoever ye do, do it heartily, as to the Lord, and not unto men.'"

Milo nodded and bent over his work, the small engraving tool making a soft buzzing sound as it etched the leather. In Daniel's arms, Emma made a small cooing sound and yawned, her tiny mouth forming a perfect O.

"She likes you," Sarah said from the doorway. "You're a natural."

Daniel looked down at the nearly sleeping baby, then back at the baseball glove taking shape under Milo's skilled hands. He thought about Will, about birthdays missed and moments lost, and about the terrifying and wonderful responsibility of being a father. Then he thought about all the birthdays to come and moments to gain, putting his focus there instead.

Later that morning the gravel driveway crunched beneath the tires as Adaline pulled up to the Matthewses' house. Before she could even turn the engine off, Mrs. Matthews appeared on the wraparound porch, her face lit with genuine warmth.

"You're here!" Mrs. Matthews called out as she slowly went down the porch steps.

Adaline had barely gotten Will's walker from the back when she found herself enveloped in one of Mrs. Matthews's signature hugs, the kind that made something deep in Adaline's chest ache with a longing she couldn't quite name.

"Will!" Mrs. Matthews released Adaline and moved to the passenger side where Will was already unbuckling his seatbelt, anxious to be free. "I am so excited for your party today!"

Will's face broke into the kind of uninhibited grin that only children could manage, the one that reminded Adaline why she kept fighting through every difficult day. "Really?"

"Well, of course," Mrs. Matthews confirmed, helping him out of the car while Adaline retrieved the rest of his belongings from the back seat.

Adaline pushed the walker around the SUV to her son, watching as he positioned himself with the practiced ease of someone who'd been navigating the world this way for years. "No one is more excited than Will. He's spoken about nothing else all week." She paused, catching Will's eye. "Except maybe baseball."

"The Prairie Dogs are going all the way this year!" Will cheered.

"How could they not with my son coaching and you pitching?" Mrs. Matthews asked.

Both women laughed, and for a moment, any anxiety Adaline may have entertained melted away, leaving her with a lightness that she rarely experienced.

"Mrs. Matthews?" Will asked, his tone of voice lifting hopefully. "Can I go visit the horses?"

Adaline felt her protective instincts flare. The farm, beautiful as it was, presented countless opportunities for Will to stumble and fall. The uneven ground, the barn with its scattered hay bales, the horses themselves—

Mrs. Matthews's hand landed on Adaline's shoulder as she addressed Will. "Pastor Matthews is out there right now. He'd love the company. And to be honest, he's still on the mend. I'd love it if you checked on him for me." She shared a look with Adaline and offered a slight wink.

"I can do that!" Will said.

Adaline nodded to herself and then to Will. "Stay with Pastor Matthews, okay? No wandering off."

"I won't! Thanks, Mom!" Will was already making his way toward the back of the house, his walker creating a rhythmic tap-slide, tap-slide against the stone pathway.

Adaline watched until he disappeared around the corner.

"He'll be fine. And so will you," Mrs. Matthews said, patting her arm.

Adaline turned her attention back to Mrs. Matthews, who was studying her with an unreadable expression. Ever since Adaline had finally confessed the truth about Daniel being Will's father, she'd been waiting for the older woman to realize what a terrible person Adaline truly was. In the moment, Mrs. Matthews had been overly kind and understanding, but Adaline wondered if that was just shock and once Mrs. Matthews processed the truth, she'd cast Adaline out of her good graces. Maybe that moment was now.

"I was just preparing lemonade for the party," Mrs. Matthews said, breaking the silence. "Why don't you join me in the kitchen? I could use an extra pair of hands."

"Sure." Adaline glanced over to the path where she'd last seen Will, her ears pricked for any sounds from him. Then she followed Mrs. Matthews up the porch steps into the house. As always, the kitchen was warm and welcoming, with herbs drying by the window and the lingering scent of something freshly baked in the air. They fell into an easy rhythm, Mrs. Matthews slicing lemons while Adaline measured sugar into a large glass pitcher.

"Is, um, Daniel around?" Adaline tried to keep her voice casual, but she felt embarrassed as soon as she asked, as if it offered insight into how she felt about him.

"No." Mrs. Matthews shook her head, her knife moving in steady, practiced strokes. "He headed out early this morning, right after caring for the animals. I'm not sure where he went." She glanced up, catching Adaline's expression. "Don't worry, dear. He wouldn't miss Will's party for anything."

The words were meant to be of comfort, but instead they drove a spike of guilt through Adaline's ribs. Daniel wouldn't miss this party, the way he had missed the previous eight. Eight birthdays, eight cake-covered smiles, eight years of watching his son grow. All missed out on because Adaline had been too afraid, too ashamed, too convinced that her secret was safer kept than told.

"Adaline." Mrs. Matthews's hand settled on her shoulder. Adaline hadn't even realized she'd stopped moving, frozen with a measuring cup suspended over the pitcher. "God is in control. He always has been."

In her heart, Adaline knew that was true. It was her mind that was always second-guessing and looking for ways to control the circumstances in her life.

Mrs. Matthews gave Adaline's shoulder a gentle squeeze before returning to her task. "When the world gives you lemons, God gives you sweet lemonade. For today, all we need to do is focus on giving Will the best birthday party ever."

"You're right," Adaline managed, her voice thick. "Regardless of how today turns out, I'm sure it will be the best birthday Will has ever had."

"Until next year's party," Mrs. Matthews said, looking up and offering a wide smile and a wink. "I'm already thinking we should do a camping theme. Will mentioned he's never been camping before."

*Next year's party.* The words hung in the air between them. Next year implied that Mrs. Matthews wouldn't be changing her tune. Will was now a permanent fixture in the Matthews family and according to Mrs. Matthews, so was Adaline.

For her entire life, Adaline had longed for belonging, roots and the sense that she wasn't drifting alone through the world. She'd convinced herself that, due to the choices she'd made, she didn't deserve the kind of happy life that others seemed to take for granted. But standing in this sun-drenched kitchen, listening to Mrs. Matthews hum the tune of "Amazing Grace" softly while she worked, something shifted in Adaline's chest. Maybe she didn't deserve it. Maybe she never would. But she was thankful for it anyway.

"I think Will would like a camping-themed birthday party next year," Adaline said softly. "That's perfect."

Daniel sat in his truck at the edge of his parents' driveway, watching through the windshield as children ran across the yard toward the decorated barn in the distance. The sound of their laughter carried on the afternoon breeze. He'd been sitting here for ten minutes, his hands gripping the steering wheel. Today would be the first of him approaching Will with the truth that Will was his son. He was Will's father.

He didn't know the first thing about being a parent. He could be a buddy, a coach, a mentor. But a father?

Daniel pushed the truck door open and reached for the carefully wrapped gift from the passenger seat. *Lord, guide me,* he prayed as he walked toward the sounds of celebration. Rounding the corner of the barn, he saw the party in full swing. Children chased each other around hay bales and parents stood in clusters with paper cups of his mom's specialty lemonade that she prepared for every birthday party that Daniel ever had when he was younger. And there, in the center of it all, was Will, his walker beside him.

Will couldn't run like the other kids, but he seemed to be enjoying watching. Then his gaze moved to where Daniel was approaching and the boy's face lit up.

"Coach Daniel! You came!"

The pure joy in Will's voice hit Daniel square in the chest.

"Sorry I'm late, sport, but I wouldn't miss your birthday party for anything."

As Daniel made his way closer, he caught sight of Adaline standing near the cake table. She was watching him with an unreadable expression. He saw the questions in her eyes and fear as well. If he had to guess, she worried that he hated her. That couldn't be further from the truth. In fact, the way he felt for her was the exact opposite.

Adaline approached him hesitantly, her hands nervously smoothing her yellow sundress. "Hi," she said softly. "Thanks for coming. I was afraid you wouldn't." The dark shadows below her eyes showed that she hadn't slept last night either.

"I wouldn't let Will down like that," he said. Even though he'd spent the entire night before praying for the strength to forgive and leaving his burden at the altar, his mind was struggling right now. He wanted to comfort Adaline and console her, but everything was still too raw.

"Daniel." His mother's voice broke through his internal struggle. "Can I speak with you for a moment?"

Daniel was grateful for the interruption because he could feel that he was about to say or do something that might deepen the pain he saw in Adaline's eyes. He followed his mother toward the edge of the party, where the noise was less overwhelming, and then she turned to face him.

"I know you're hurting," she said, her tone gentle. "And, son, you have every right to be."

He looked at his mother's face and realized she knew. "Mom, I missed so much," he said quietly. "Nine years of his life. His first steps, his first words. I don't even know what his first word was." He raked a hand through his hair. "I wasn't there for any of it."

"No, you weren't," she agreed. "It's going to take time to grieve those lost moments. But Daniel, you're here now. Today, you get to watch your son celebrate his birthday surrounded by friends who love him. Today, you get to start building a relationship with him. You don't have his past, but you do have the present. And the future."

"I know. You don't need to be concerned about me making a scene. I don't want to lash out or hurt Adaline."

Relief was reflected in his mother's posture. She reached out and placed a hand on his forearm. "You have matured so much. I am so proud of you, son."

Her words meant a lot to him. Daniel hadn't even realized that some part of him had wondered if his parents were proud. He'd actually thought that they'd see this as one more way he'd let them down.

"Coach Daniel, are you gonna stay for cake?" Will asked, making his way toward them. "Your mom made it, and it's chocolate with vanilla frosting. It's my favorite."

"I wouldn't miss it." Daniel headed toward Will, not wanting him to wear himself out walking along the uneven terrain. "But first, I have something for you."

Will's eyes widened as Daniel handed him a wrapped package. "Can I open it now?"

"It's your birthday. You can open it whenever you want."

Daniel watched as Will carefully unwrapped the gift, his small fingers working to preserve the paper in a way that suggested Adaline had taught him to be thoughtful about such things. When the wrapping fell away, Will let out an audible gasp.

"A baseball mitt!"

Daniel had purchased a perfectly sized mitt for Will's hand and had gotten Milo to engrave a Bible verse.

Will ran his finger along the words as he read. "Colossians 3:23. And whatsoever ye do, do it heartily, as to the Lord, and not unto men."

Will slipped the mitt onto his hand. "This is the best present ever! Look, it fits perfectly!"

"Do you know what that verse means?" Daniel's mother asked. "It means that whether you're playing baseball or doing your homework or helping your mom, you should always do your best because God is watching and He's proud of you."

Will nodded solemnly, clearly taking the lesson to heart. "I'm gonna wear this every single day. Can we practice with it after the party?" he asked Daniel.

"Sure, buddy," Daniel promised.

"Yes! I need to go show my mom," he said excitedly, turning to head back in the direction that he'd come from.

Daniel chuckled as his gaze followed Will. Then he realized that Adaline was watching from a few yards away. Their eyes met again, and this time, Daniel didn't look away. His heart had forgiven last night, but he needed his mind to catch up. Forgiveness was a choice, but it was also an action. It was a smile, a wave.

He offered both from where he stood and felt the distance close just slightly. Even still, he started walking in the opposite direction, needing to clear his mind.

This whole situation felt like a dream that he was going to wake up from. Just the other night while coaching the kids on the baseball field, he'd thought to himself how wonderful it would be to be a dad one day. Watching the boys with their fathers made his memories of him and his own dad come back. Daniel's father had been amazing, in his opinion. He'd always made time for Daniel, whether it was to practice pitching or to go fishing. And without fail, his father always weaved in a sermon on the side for good measure.

*Thank You, God, that Dad is on the mend. Thank You for Your healing and restoration*, Daniel prayed, walking toward the stable where Star was waiting in her stall. Some part of Daniel had been holding his breath during this illness his father had just come out of. Carlos's accident in high school had taught Daniel that life was fragile and tomorrow wasn't promised. It was a hard lesson, but one that everyone learned along the way.

Now Daniel was a father. He didn't feel like one though. He'd already missed so many moments. Would he ever catch up? Could he be the kind of dad that he'd had growing up?

# *Chapter Thirteen*

Adaline stood near the refreshment table, refilling cups of lemonade, but her attention was entirely focused on Daniel and Will on the far side of the farm. Daniel was crouched down beside Will, adjusting his stance as he prepared to swing at a baseball placed on a batting tee.

When Will connected with the ball and sent it flying toward the barn, Daniel lifted both arms and cheered, the sound covering the entire farm. He lifted Will up and jogged toward the makeshift first base. Then Will tagged a peer runner who raced through the rest of the bases the way they did at Little League practice. All the children cheered as the peer runner completed the home run, acknowledging Will as much as the other child.

This was what Adaline had dreamed of for Will. She wanted him to be included despite his physical challenges. She wanted others to celebrate his victories even though they were small in comparison to what other children could do. She also wanted Will to have a father figure. A father.

She found herself studying Daniel's interactions with all the children, not just Will. He made each child feel special, finding something to encourage in every attempt. His patience and gentle way were the same qualities that had drawn her to him in high school. When her confidence had been at its lowest, he'd shown her the beauty that he saw in her. Not just physical beauty but he'd acknowledged how she made others smile and her way with words.

Watching him now, it was easy to remember why Adaline had fallen so hard for him all those years ago. He had a heart for others and he made everyone around him want to be better than they were.

Would he ever be that way with her again?

Earlier, when she'd thanked him for coming to the party, he hadn't been cold exactly, but he certainly wasn't his normal friendly self either. The distance in his voice had made it clear that he was still upset, and rightfully so. She just didn't know how to fix this.

"Coach Daniel is the best!" she heard Will declare to a group of his classmates as they gathered around the water fountain. "He taught me how to hold the bat so I can hit the ball every time, and he says I have natural talent!"

Adaline's heart soared and broke simultaneously. Will had already bonded so completely with his biological father, and he didn't even know that's what Daniel was. The irony was almost too much to bear.

"Quite a scene, isn't it?"

Adaline turned to find Tammy approaching with a knowing smile. Will had invited Brian, who was his peer runner on the team.

"It really is," Adaline agreed, forcing herself to focus on the conversation. "The kids are having such a wonderful time."

Tammy followed Adaline's gaze to where Daniel was now organizing a three-legged race, pairing children strategically to ensure everyone could participate successfully. "That Daniel Matthews is quite something, isn't he? I have to say, he was a topic of interest at the single moms support group last night," she said. "Not because the others wanted to date him, but because he's been making such a difference with the kids. He's a good male role model."

"Oh?"

"Yep. I hear he's thinking about taking over the youth group at church too."

Adaline hadn't heard that, but it didn't surprise her. Daniel really did have a natural talent with kids.

"Anyway, happy birthday to your son. Will is such a special boy. And you are a super mom."

"Me?" Adaline asked with surprise.

"Yes, you. Look at how well-adjusted he is despite all of his health stuff and losing his father at such a young age."

Adaline nodded, not trusting herself to speak. It was true. Will had been through much more than most kids his age and he was amazingly resilient.

Tammy tipped her head toward another parent. "Did you hear about poor Madison? Her ex is trying to take full custody of her son. I can't imagine what that would feel like," Tammy said. "From what I hear the whole situation is turning into an absolute nightmare."

The words reignited Adaline's worst fear. What if Daniel decided to petition the court for custody of Will? What if his hurt and anger over her betrayal led him to believe that she was an unfit mother and that Will would be better off with him and his parents? After keeping his son from him for nine years, Daniel might be angry enough to pursue exactly that kind of revenge.

The thought made Adaline physically sick. The idea of having their little family torn apart by legal battles and custody arrangements was too much to bear.

"Adaline? Are you all right?" Tammy's voice seemed to come from very far away.

"Yes. I'm fine," Adaline managed, though her voice sounded strained even to her own ears. "Just thinking about…things."

Tammy followed her gaze back to Daniel, who was now helping Will navigate the three-legged race with another child. "You know," she said thoughtfully, "I've always thought you and Daniel would make your way back to one another."

"That was so long ago," Adaline said quickly. The last thing she needed was Tammy speculating about her relationship with Daniel. Tammy was nice, but if she was discussing other people's custody battles, then she would probably pass on whatever Adaline told her right now.

"The past," Tammy repeated knowingly. "You know, the thing about the past is, if there wasn't closure, it's not closed."

Adaline let that bit of wisdom sink in. There definitely wasn't closure with what she had had with Daniel.

As Tammy moved away to check on her own son, Adaline found herself sending up a silent prayer. *I know I've made terrible mistakes, and I know I don't deserve his friendship. But please don't let my failures cost Will the father he's always needed. And please don't let it cost Will his mother.* Will needed both her and Daniel in his life. Even if Daniel never looked at her romantically again, she hoped they'd find a way to be peaceful co-parents for Will's sake.

Across the yard, Daniel looked up and caught her watching him. For just a moment, their eyes met and held. Adaline searched his expression, looking for any hint at how he was feeling toward her. But Daniel's expression remained carefully neutral before he turned his attention back to the children. On a sigh, Adaline wrapped her arms around herself, suddenly feeling cold despite the warm midday sun. Today was a day for celebrating, but her heart was finding it difficult to feel the joy.

* * *

Paper plates and plastic cups littered the tables and streamers hung askew from fence posts as Daniel gathered the remnants of what had been a great birthday party, at least in his opinion. He'd watched his son celebrate his ninth birthday surrounded by friends who clearly loved him. Will's face had lit up with each gift, and the laughter that rang out all afternoon still echoed in Daniel's mind as he dutifully cleaned up the back yard.

"Coach Daniel?" Will's voice interrupted his thoughts. He was sitting on a bale of hay, carefully inspecting the baseball mitt that Daniel had given him. "Are you gonna keep being my friend after the Little League season is over?"

The question hit Daniel squarely in the chest. There was something vulnerable in Will's voice, a hint of the insecurity that probably came from having other people in his life come and go.

Daniel abandoned his cleanup efforts and walked over to sit beside Will. "I'm not going anywhere. Friends don't disappear just because a season ends, and I plan on being your friend for a very long time."

"You do?"

"Definitely. In fact, I was hoping you might want to keep practicing pitching and catching even after the season's over. Maybe work on some new skills for next year."

"That would be so cool! I want to get really good so I can maybe play on the middle school team someday. Do you think they'd let me use my walker and have all the things you allow?"

Daniel wasn't sure of school sports regulations, but if he had any say, Will would have the necessary accommodations to do anything he set his mind to. "I think if you practice, you'll keep improving, and I will go to bat for you whenever you need me to."

Spontaneously, Will leaned in and wrapped his arm around Daniel. "You're such a good coach. You're the best!"

Daniel loved being Will's coach, but he wanted more. He needed it. At some point, he and Adaline would have to have an honest conversation about co-parenting arrangements. The casual promises he was making to Will weren't something he could deliver on without Adaline's cooperation, and more importantly, he wanted Will to know that his presence was permanent, not dependent on the whims of a baseball schedule.

"Daniel, thank you so much for helping to clean up."

He looked up to see Adaline approaching, her arms full of folded tablecloths and her cheeks flushed from the afternoon sun. She'd changed from her party dress into jeans and a simple T-shirt.

"It's no problem," Daniel said, standing as she reached them. "The party was amazing, Addie. You did a wonderful job."

"Me? Your mom did almost everything." Adaline set down the tablecloths and reached out to touch his arm lightly. "I can't tell you how much I appreciate your parents' generosity. Will wanted to have his party on the farm with the horses, but I think Will and the rest of the kids were more enamored with Coach Daniel than Star."

Despite everything that had happened between them, despite the hurt that still sat like a stone in his chest, Daniel didn't pull away from her touch. He was making an active choice for his body language to match his heart. He didn't resent her. He forgave her, despite the hurt that he knew would take a while to lessen.

And he cared about her well-being. She was the mother

of his son after all, but it was more than that. He just wasn't ready to explore how much more.

"Mom, look how perfectly my mitt fits!" Will interrupted his thoughts, holding up his hand to display the new glove. "Coach Daniel, you should see my mom try to pitch a baseball. She's really not very good at it."

Adaline laughed and covered her face with one hand in embarrassment. "Will Harper, you're not supposed to tell people about your mother's athletic shortcomings."

Harper.

Daniel knew that Will didn't have his last name, but he hadn't really considered it until this moment. There were so many things to consider.

"But it's true, Mom!" Will grinned at both of them. "I've been asking her to practice with me in the yard, and she throws like…like…" He searched for an appropriately dramatic comparison.

"Like someone who's never played baseball?" Adaline supplied with good humor.

"Exactly! Coach Daniel, maybe you could teach my mom how to pitch properly too. Then she could help me practice when you're not around."

Daniel shared a look with Adaline. Her smile slid away and questions filled her eyes. Yeah, they needed to talk and soon.

"Will, Coach Daniel is very busy," she said quickly, giving Daniel an easy out. "I'm just grateful that he's taking the time to help you learn about baseball. I can figure out how to throw a ball properly on my own."

Daniel watched her fumble with the tablecloth, clearly flustered by her son's suggestion.

"Please, Coach Daniel," Will pressed, oblivious to the tension. "Teach my mom to pitch. Then we could have our own team!"

The innocent excitement in Will's voice made Daniel's chest tighten. What would happen when he knew that Daniel was his real father? Daniel imagined that Will would start dreaming of them all becoming one big happy family. How could Daniel crush that dream?

"Maybe I could give your mom a few pointers after the Little League season is over," Daniel heard himself saying. "If she wants to learn, that is."

Will's face brightened. "That would be so awesome! Mom, you could be a Prairie Dog next year."

Adaline looked at Daniel with something akin to gratitude. "I think I might be too old to be a Prairie Dog. It's too late for me," she said on a small laugh.

"Nah," Daniel disagreed. "It's never too late."

A meaningful look crossed between them. He wasn't just talking about baseball, he realized. Whatever complications lay ahead in his relationship with Adaline, Will's well-being had to come first. And if that meant pretending that teaching Adaline to pitch was purely about baseball rather than an excuse to spend time together, then so be it. Healing took time, but he was willing if she was.

"We're going to have so much fun!" Will declared. "This is my favorite birthday!"

Adaline's eyes were suddenly shiny. Looking at Daniel again, she mouthed a thank-you.

He was the grateful one though. She didn't have to tell him. She could have kept the secret for the rest of her life. This was a gift for him. The best gift he could have ever received.

# *Chapter Fourteen*

The next morning, Adaline patiently guided Will down the church's aisle toward their usual spot, where they'd sat every Sunday since Adaline had joined the church.

They were almost to their pew when Adaline sensed a shift in the air and realized that Daniel was approaching. Her heart quickened and her breaths became shallower.

"Morning." Daniel's voice was carefully neutral as he stopped beside them.

"Hi, Coach Daniel!" Will's greeting held none of the awkwardness that stretched between the adults. His face lit up the way it always did when he saw Daniel.

"Hey, buddy. How's the birthday boy feeling today?"

"My birthday was yesterday, Coach," Will said. "Today is the Lord's day and I feel great! Mom let me eat leftover cake for breakfast."

Heat crept up through Adaline's neck. Good mothers made healthy breakfasts, especially on Sunday mornings. "It was a small piece," she said, wanting to slink into the pews.

Daniel's lips twitched in a not-quite smile. At least the moment relieved some of the tension between them, but not completely.

"Coach Daniel, can we sit with you?" Will asked. "I've never sat in the front row."

Adaline's mind raced through a dozen different responses.

Sitting with the pastor's son on the front row would be the talk of all the congregants for the rest of the week ahead. As if the congregation wasn't already buzzing with speculation about why Daniel Matthews was still in town and whether he had taken an interest in Adaline again. Just last week, Mrs. Henderson had cornered Adaline in the grocery store, fishing for information for her book club.

Adaline opened her mouth, scrambling for a gentle way to say no, but Daniel spoke first.

"You know what, Will?" He crouched down slightly, bringing himself to eye level with the boy. "My mom is pretty strict in church. When I was growing up, I couldn't move without getting the look from her." He widened his eyes in exaggerated fear.

"The look?" Will asked.

Adaline couldn't help but laugh. At least that boded well in how Daniel perceived her motherhood. The fact that Will didn't know "the look" was a testimony to her patience.

"Oh, yeah." Daniel nodded with all seriousness. "Lowered brows. Narrowed eyes. The slightest turn of her face so that those eyes slid to the farthest corner." He demonstrated the expression as he described it, making Adaline laugh harder. "Trust me, buddy," Daniel finally said, "unless you're a statue and can sit very still the full hour, you don't want to sit in the same pew as my mother."

Will giggled, and Daniel glanced up at Adaline. Their eyes met, and Adaline perceived a different look. Despite all the unresolved tension between them, he still made her feel like that giddy teenage girl she'd been at eighteen. The one who'd thought Daniel Matthews hung the moon and stars. That was in her BC era, before she'd started going to church and learned who really put that moon and those stars in the sky.

A smile tugged at her cheeks before she could stop it.

"I'll come find you after church, though," Daniel said, straightening up. "Maybe we can play catch with that new mitt of yours in the church field for a few minutes?"

"Really?" Will's entire face transformed with joy.

"Really." Daniel's hand rested briefly on Will's shoulder, and Adaline saw the longing in that gesture. He wanted to show up as a father. "And, Adaline, I want to ask you something after church, too."

Her heart stuttered. "Oh. Okay."

Daniel waved and continued toward the front pew, where his mother was already seated. Adaline and Will settled into their usual pew. Over the next hour, Adaline tried and failed to focus on Pastor Jason's sermon about grace; her mind kept drifting to Daniel's words. What did he want to ask? Was it good? Bad? Had he decided he wanted to go ahead and tell Will the truth? Had his parents convinced him that Adaline was a lost cause and not worth the complication?

Beside her, Will fidgeted constantly, adjusting his position, swinging one foot, whispering questions about when church would be over. Adaline found herself thinking that Mrs. Matthews probably would have given him "the look" by now. Maybe Daniel had been protecting them both with his excuse.

When Pastor Jason finally wrapped up the sermon and said the closing prayer, Adaline stood on autopilot, helping Will position himself behind his walker. Through the crowd of parishioners filing toward the exits, she spotted Daniel making his way toward them, his tall frame easy to track.

Her heartbeat quickened. Maybe he wanted to invite them to lunch at the Matthewses' home. Sunday lunch at the farm, where she could pretend, just for a few hours, that they were a real family. She'd say yes to the invitation. If he asked. The answer was already forming on her lips.

"Hey, Will." Daniel reached them, his hand finding Will's shoulder again with that same careful affection. Then his eyes lifted to Adaline. "Can I talk to you alone for a second?"

"Oh, um, yeah. Sure." He hadn't needed her alone when he'd invited her to lunch before. What if he only wanted Will to go to lunch at his parents? What if he was slowly pushing Adaline out of the picture?

She stepped to the side, far enough that Will couldn't hear but close enough to keep him in her peripheral vision. Daniel followed, and suddenly they were standing closer than they'd been since the afternoon of the party, since their argument, since everything had gotten so tense.

Adaline looked up at him. He didn't look mad or like he was about to exclude her from a lunch invitation. Maybe he wanted to talk about them. About what they'd been and what they could be again. This wasn't the time or place for that though.

"Addie, I want to take Will out on Dad's boat next Saturday morning," Daniel said. "I want to teach him to fish."

The words hit her like a splash of cold water. "What?"

"I know it's short notice, but the weather's perfect and I just thought—"

"On a boat?" Adaline's voice climbed higher than she intended. "Daniel, he can't swim. He's never been on a boat. I've never let him—"

"I know." Daniel's jaw tightened. "But I'm his father, Addie. I want to teach my son to fish."

*I'm his father.* The words reverberated through her chest, each syllable a reminder of everything she'd stolen from Daniel, from Will, from all of them. Nine years of moments she could never give back. Nine years of firsts she'd denied the father of her only child.

Her heart pounded so hard she could feel it in her throat.

Will had never been out of her sight for any real length of time. She'd held him close, protected him, controlled every variable she could because the world was dangerous and he was so vulnerable.

And she was all he had.

Except he wasn't all hers anymore. And maybe he never should have been.

"Addie?" Daniel's voice softened. "I'll keep him safe. I promise."

*God help me*, she prayed silently, desperately. *Give me the strength to let go.*

She looked up at Daniel, and her vision blurred with tears she hadn't realized were forming. Every instinct screamed at her to say no, to keep Will close, to maintain the control that had kept them safe—if isolated—for nine years.

But she had no right. Not anymore. Maybe she never had.

"I'm not sure," she said. "I'll, um, I'll let you know."

Disappointment reflected in Daniel's eyes. Even so, he didn't argue. "Thanks, Adaline." The use of her whole name instead of the shortened version stung. Turning, Daniel stepped over to where Will was and patted his back. Then he started to walk away.

"Daniel?" Adaline called out, stopping him in his tracks.

He turned to look at her. Low brows. Narrowed eyes. His head slightly angled. He wasn't happy with her right now and she couldn't blame him.

"Yes." She nodded quickly, on the verge of tears. "About next Saturday. My answer is yes."

The following Saturday, the early-morning mist hung over Prairie Lake like a soft gray blanket.

"I can't believe my mom said yes to this!" Will said for the third time since Daniel had picked him up this morning.

They were on Daniel's father's small boat that Daniel regularly took out when he was home. Will had on a life vest and he was buckled in to the boat's passenger seat beside him, his face bright with excitement despite the early hour.

Honestly, Daniel couldn't believe that Adaline had agreed either.

"I'll take good care of him, I promise," he'd said as he picked Will up this morning. "Fishing was my favorite pastime at Will's age," he'd added, seeing Adaline's worry shift to guilt.

"Mom never lets me go anywhere this early on Saturday mornings," Will continued, rocking the boat slightly with his boisterous movements and likely scaring off all the fish. "Usually we're doing laundry and cleaning my room."

Daniel smiled as he baited Will's hook. "Well, the fish bite better in the morning when it's quiet and peaceful. Plus, your mom knows I'll take good care of you." Daniel understood that it wouldn't be easy for her to loosen her grip, but the more she saw that he was perfectly capable, the easier it'd be. And hopefully, with time, the tension in the air between them would ease. He didn't want to resent the mother of his child. He wanted to be friends and partners, the way two parents should.

"Have you been fishing here since you were a kid?" Will watched intently as Daniel demonstrated how to cast the line.

"Ever since I was about your age, actually. My dad used to bring me out on this lake every Saturday morning during the summer." Daniel settled into the boat's built-in seat and cast his line into the water. "We'd talk about baseball, school or sometimes just sit quietly and watch the sun rise over the water."

Will's smile dipped into a subtle frown.

"What's wrong, bud?" Daniel asked.

"I just... Well, sometimes I wish I had a dad. Mine died when I was two."

Daniel empathized. According to Adaline, Christopher had treated Will just like his own flesh and blood. He was a father in all the ways that counted, and Daniel could never repay him for giving his son a father's love while he was alive. "I'm sorry about that, buddy."

Will looked over at him. "It's not your fault." He shrugged. "My dad loved God and Jesus so I know he's okay. I just wish I could have had more time with him to do stuff like you did with your dad growing up." Will attempted to replicate what Daniel had done, pulling back his pole and pushing it forward quickly to cast. He wasn't as strong or coordinated though, and the line didn't go out as far as Daniel's had. It landed in the water with a satisfying plop, creating a tiny circle on the water's surface that expanded out until it was a larger circle.

"Way to go," Daniel said in a low tone of voice to keep from scaring away the fish.

Then they sat and waited, watching their lines and listening to the morning sounds of the lake awakening.

"Look!" Will said loudly after a moment, lifting one arm to point across the lake. "A blue heron!"

Daniel couldn't help but laugh at the thought of all the fish that might have been en route to their lines, changing direction and swimming away. "I see it," he said in a whisper voice. "Remember, we have to keep our voices low. The fish can hear us, you know."

Will grimaced. "Sorry. I forgot. It's hard because I can't see them."

Daniel remembered a similar conversation he'd had with his own father at Will's age. He glanced around the lake and pointed. "See that little circle in the water over there?"

Will squinted his eyes and looked for what Daniel was referring to. "I see it," he finally said, keeping his voice softer this time.

"We can't see the fish, but if we look real hard, we can see the evidence of them. Kind of like God. We don't see Him, but the evidence is everywhere."

Will's wide grin revealed a missing tooth in the lower back corner. "Coach Daniel?" he asked after another long moment of quiet waiting. "Are you and my mom friends?"

Daniel was surprised by the question. "Yes. I'd say that's true."

Will seemed to chew on this thought for a while. "She's a really great mom. She'd probably make a great wife too."

There was nothing subtle about where Will was going with this conversation. "Your mother has enough on her plate right now."

"She has too much," Will corrected. "That's why she needs a husband."

Daniel didn't want to pop Will's bubble or give him false hope. "You stick to fishing for fish and let God hook your mom a husband, if and when the time is right. Okay, sport?"

Will looked out on the water for a long moment. "Pastor Matthews says that God needs help sometimes. That's why people serve in the church."

Daniel chuckled, the sound carrying across the still water and likely spooking all the fish again. He patted Will's shoulder. "Persistence is going to get you far in life, son."

Son. It was a term of endearment, but it was also the truth.

"You and my mom dated a long time ago, right? That's what my friend Carson told me."

Daniel glanced over. "Yes, we did."

Will ignored his fishing pole now. "Do you still think my mom is pretty?"

The question nearly knocked Daniel off the boat. "Yes," he said honestly. "Your mom is very pretty."

"I knew it! You should marry her so I can have a second dad. And not just any dad—the coolest dad in town!"

*Oh, boy.* He didn't want Will getting his hopes up, though it seemed to be too late for that.

"Just because I know about baseball and fishing doesn't mean I know about leading a family. Those are very different skills."

Will shook his head, his smile never wavering. "God will help you figure it out, Coach. All you have to do is ask Him."

This child had more wisdom in his nine-year-old heart than Daniel had managed to accumulate in thirty years of living. Well, that wasn't necessarily true. Daniel had always had faith and belief but he'd let his sin anchor him and keep him from the freedom that Jesus already bought and paid for.

"Mom always says that God has the gifts and the plan. We don't need to know how or why—we just need to listen to Him. That's why I wasn't afraid when I felt like God wanted me to play baseball."

Daniel raised a brow. "Yeah?"

Will nodded. "I had a dream that I was playing baseball. I woke up and started to cry when I realized it wasn't real." Will shook his head. "But then I opened my Bible later that day and I saw the verse that my mom highlighted for me a long time ago. All things are possible for those who love Him." Will shrugged. "Pastor Matthews says that God's promises are real. If that's the case, then I knew that I could play baseball too. And you can be a cool dad," Will added.

Daniel looked at his son's earnest face. This boy was so innocent and his faith was so strong. Maybe Will was right. All things were possible, even fixing a broken family and making it whole.

# *Chapter Fifteen*

*Lord, give me strength.*

Two weeks had passed since Adaline told Daniel the truth about him being Will's father. That, in and of itself, was a huge step toward personal growth. Tonight Adaline was taking another step, assuming she actually opened her car door and walked into Prairie Community Church.

Over the past year, Adaline had been invited to the Single Mothers Support Group so many times, but she'd always made excuses. Tonight, however, she felt an irresistible pull. She'd been trying to handle everything alone for too long. Raising a child took a village—isn't that what everyone liked to say? Raising a child with disabilities maybe took more than a village. She understood that now. It took both parents, ideally, grandparents and a church family.

Having caring friends like Beth who didn't mind watching Will for an hour was helpful, too. Adaline could have asked Daniel, but things had been awkward between them since Will's party and then the fishing trip that Adaline hadn't wanted to agree to. She and Daniel needed to sit down, alone, and have an honest conversation. Their roles had changed and so had the rules. Until they sat down for a no-holds-barred discussion, neither knew how to act or even feel.

Taking a deep breath, Adaline grabbed her purse and walked toward the church fellowship hall. Through the windows, she could see a circle of chairs occupied by women of various ages. She recognized most of them from around the town. Some even worked at the same school where she did. A coffeepot percolated loudly on a side table next to a plate of homemade cookies filling the room with a welcoming aroma.

"Adaline!" Tammy Richardson lifted a hand to get Adaline's attention. Then she popped up from her chair and headed in Adaline's direction. "I'm so glad you decided to join us tonight. Come sit by me." She grabbed Adaline's hand and gently tugged toward where she'd been sitting.

As Adaline settled into the circle, she felt both vulnerable and relieved. These women understood the unique challenges of raising children alone, the weight of making every decision without a partner, the exhaustion of being both mother and father to their kids.

"We were just sharing updates about our week," explained Margaret Davis, a widow with three teenage daughters. "Would you like to tell us what brought you here tonight?"

Adaline hesitated, then remembered Jason's counsel about letting go of control and trusting others. "I realized that I've been trying to do everything by myself for too long. My son, Will, has cerebral palsy, and between his therapy appointments, school activities and just daily life, I sometimes feel like I'm drowning. I thought coming here might help me figure out how to...well, how to not carry everything alone."

The murmurs of understanding around the circle made her chest feel lighter. These women understood the bone-deep tiredness, the constant worry and the isolation that came with single parenthood.

"Oh, honey, we've all been there," Tammy said, reaching over to squeeze Adaline's hand. "When my oldest, Tim, was Will's age, I was convinced that I had to handle everything myself. It nearly broke me before I learned to accept help."

"What kind of help do you need most?" another mother, Lisa Chen, asked. Lisa's twin boys were notorious for their energy. "Carpooling? Babysitting? Meal trains? We're pretty good at organizing practical support around here."

Adaline felt tears prick her eyes at the immediate offers of assistance. "Honestly, just knowing I'm not the only one struggling helps more than you know. But...maybe carpooling to some of Will's activities? Baseball practice is twice a week, and therapy is once a week. It would be nice to not always be the one driving."

"Consider it done," one mother said immediately. "Tommy and Will are on the same team anyway. I can easily pick up Will on my practice days."

The easy generosity overwhelmed Adaline. For years, she'd been so focused on proving she could handle everything alone that she'd forgotten the blessing of community. Some part of her didn't want to accept help though because of Will's physical needs. But he had made so much progress that she knew he could advocate for himself.

"I have something else I wanted to share," Adaline said, surprising herself with her boldness. "I've been working on a children's book. It's about a little boy with a disability similar to Will's, and how he discovers that God made him special for a reason."

Excitement rippled through the group.

"Oh, Adaline, that's wonderful!" exclaimed one of the women. "My youngest daughter has been asking me how she should interact with Will at school. She wants to be his friend but doesn't know if it's okay to ask about his walker or if she should pretend not to notice it."

"My son asked me the same thing," added Tammy. "I struggled with what to tell him because honestly, I was never taught how to talk to children about disabilities. A book like that would be such a gift to families like ours."

Lisa nodded enthusiastically. "There's such a need for books that help typical children understand that they can ask questions and be friends with kids who are different. It would help Will too, knowing that other children are learning about acceptance and inclusion."

The validation filled Adaline with a confidence she hadn't felt in years. Maybe Will's story really could help other families navigate similar challenges.

As the evening progressed, the conversation naturally turned to relationships and the complexities of dating as single mothers. Some women shared stories of second chances they'd found in love; others talked about the challenges of introducing new partners to their children.

"I keep telling myself I'll think about dating when my kids are older," admitted another mother. "But sometimes I wonder if that's fair to any of us. They need to see what a healthy relationship looks like, and I…well, I miss having a life partner. You know, someone to tell everything in my day to."

"I used to think the same way," said Tammy. "But then I realized I was putting my life on hold indefinitely. There's nothing wrong with wanting companionship and love. God created man for woman and vice versa. He created marriage."

Adaline found herself thinking about Daniel and about the way her heart had awakened from years of dormancy the moment she'd seen him again. She'd felt nothing remotely similar since they'd dated in high school, not even during her marriage to Chris. Daniel had been her first love, and apparently her only true love.

"What about you, Adaline?" asked Jennifer gently. "Are you open to finding love again?"

Adaline's face grew hot. She wasn't used to sharing such personal things with others. She wanted to though. The group felt welcoming and nonjudgmental. "There's…someone, I guess. Someone from my past who's recently returned. It's complicated though. I made mistakes and I'm not sure he can forgive me."

"Honey," Tammy said gently, "the Bible tells us in Isaiah, chapter 43, to forget the former things and not dwell on the past, because God is doing a new thing."

Another mother nodded and added, "And 1 John 1:9 reminds us that if we confess our sins, He is faithful and just to forgive us. If God can forgive us, maybe this man can too."

Lisa leaned forward toward Adaline. "Sometimes we have to be brave enough to believe we deserve a second chance. Your son needs to see you fighting for happiness, not just accepting whatever scraps life hands you."

As the meeting wound down and the women began to clean up, Adaline felt something she hadn't experienced in years. Hope. And Peace.

Walking to her car under the star-filled sky, she lifted up a silent prayer.

*Lord, I don't know what You have planned for Daniel and me. I know I don't deserve his forgiveness, and I know I've made mistakes that hurt him deeply. But if there's any chance for us to be a family, the family Will deserves, please make a way. Help me trust Your timing and Your plan.*

As she drove home, Adaline allowed herself to imagine a different future. One where she didn't have to carry every burden alone, where Will had the father he needed and where love got a second chance to bloom.

God really was doing a new thing. She could feel it. And for the first time in years, she was ready for change instead of scared of it.

* * *

The faces on the young adults in the room were a blend of excitement and disinterest. Daniel searched every one, hoping that he could be the mentor they needed. He was also a bit nervous. The last time he'd sat in this position, he'd been their same age. Now he was the old guy in the room and he knew that's what some of them were thinking.

Even though he had changed, the familiar space was exactly how he remembered. The same worn carpet, the same mismatched chairs, the same cross hanging on the wall. In those mismatched chairs sat the children of the friends he'd grown up with. There was Eva, the assistant pastor's daughter. Jake, whose mother had been praying for his salvation since he'd started running with the "wrong crowd." Sarah, who Jason had confided battled anxiety and depression. These kids deserved a leader who was worthy of their trust, and Daniel couldn't shake the feeling that he fell short.

God didn't though. Maybe he wasn't worthy, but God put him here for a reason just as He had so many years ago.

"Welcome, everyone," Daniel began, his voice steadier than he felt. "For those who don't know me, I'm Daniel Matthews. I used to lead this youth group about ten years ago, before I left for college."

What he didn't say was how he'd left the youth group at their age, grief-stricken and angry at God after losing his friend. He'd strayed from the path he'd always faithfully walked and foolishly done things he knew went against God and the Bible's teaching.

"Tonight, I thought we'd talk about mistakes." Daniel settled into a chair among the teenagers rather than standing above them. "And about how God can use even our worst failures for His glory. If we allow Him to."

The discussion started slowly, with typical teenage reluctance to participate. But gradually, they began to share their struggles with peer pressure, battles with addiction and the constant pressure to fit in while trying to follow Christ.

Jake, the sixteen-year-old boy whose mother worriedly told Daniel he was hanging out with poor influences, cleared his throat and spoke in a barely audible whisper. "My parents are getting a divorce. I've kind of been going through a rough spot."

"I'm sorry to hear that," Daniel said.

Jake shrugged. "I'm kind of mad, you know. Sometimes I'm mad at God even. How can I be a Christian when I can't even control my thoughts?"

The raw pain in Jake's voice hit Daniel like a physical blow. He saw himself at that age and recalled the exact same conviction. The room fell silent, waiting for Daniel's response.

He hadn't planned to share his own story tonight, but looking at Jake's anguished expression, Daniel knew he needed to give these youth more than surface-level encouragement.

"Jake," Daniel said quietly, "let me tell you about the time I turned my back on God."

And then, following the gentle nudge in his heart, Daniel told them everything. He spoke about Carlos's accident and praying that God would heal his friend. About his hurt and anger when that didn't happen. He stopped praying. Stopped reading his Bible. Daniel didn't want to go to church anymore. "I stopped turning to God for comfort," he told the group. "At first I was mad at God and that's why I stayed away. Then, as my heart healed, I felt ashamed. I didn't feel worthy to come before Him."

As he spoke, Daniel watched the teenagers' faces transform. The judgment he'd expected wasn't there. Instead, he saw recognition, relief and hope. His failures were becoming a powerful testimony. His story was proof that God's grace could cover even the deepest shame.

"The thing is," Daniel continued, his voice growing stronger, "I may have turned my back on God, but He never turned from me. I spent years believing that my mistakes had disqualified me from serving God. But God doesn't see our failures the way we do. He sees the potential for a testimony that can help others who are struggling with the same things."

Eva raised her hand tentatively. "What if someone can't forgive you? What if your mistakes hurt other people and they won't give you a second chance?"

Adaline came to mind. He knew he'd hurt her first by breaking her trust and her heart. Even so, he was struggling to come to terms with all his lost time with Will. His son. Since Will's party, Daniel had found himself laughing and his guard lowering as he talked to Adaline at church or after baseball practice. Then he'd remember what she'd done and he'd feel his heart harden.

"I'm actually struggling with unforgiveness right now," Daniel admitted. "Someone I care about made choices that hurt me deeply. And I've been holding onto that hurt. Not intentionally. I'm trying to let go, but I'll be honest with you guys. It's not easy. Not on your own, at least."

Sarah's young face was serious. "My mom always says that holding onto anger is like drinking poison and expecting the other person to get sick."

"Your mom's a wise woman," Daniel said. "The truth is, holding onto hurt is exactly what the enemy wants for us. Unforgiveness becomes a barrier that keeps us from the love and relationships God wants to give us."

As the conversation continued, with teenagers sharing their own struggles with forgiveness and grace, Daniel felt a shift in his heart. That was the power of Christian fellowship, and these teens needed it as much as, or more, than anyone.

Daniel had needed it at their age. For a long time after Carlos's death, he'd been angry at God. Then when the grief settled and his anger faded, he was left with immense shame over not having strong enough faith to endure instead of stray. God was using Daniel's past tonight to help these teenagers though. Maybe more than one.

Jake spoke up again. "What if the person who's hurt you doesn't even want your forgiveness? They aren't even sorry. How do you forgive someone when you know they don't care about what they did, and you don't feel like forgiving them?"

"Unforgiveness is a sin. Plain and simple. You don't need an apology to decide to forgive. Forgiveness is a choice, Jake. Give your pain to God and then go through the motions. Pray for the person who hurt you and mean it. Ask God to change your heart toward them," Daniel said, soaking in his own advice. Adaline had allowed him to take Will on another fishing outing on Friday night while she attended a church group. This one on land at a little pond in the park. It was only an hour and a half, but that time meant everything to Daniel. He wanted to tell Will the truth. He was ready to fully step into the role of being Will's father, but it was clear that Adaline wasn't. For now, he was being patient and trying not to resent her hesitation. "Sometimes you have to make the decision to forgive over and over again until your heart finally believes what your mind knows to be true."

As the meeting wound down, Daniel led the group in prayer and then saw each one leave with their ride. Then he sat alone in the room for a moment, reflecting on everything that had happened in tonight's group. He felt in his heart that this was where he was meant to serve right now. These kids needed him. And he needed them too.

# *Chapter Sixteen*

Adaline closed her lesson plan book Monday afternoon and rubbed her tired eyes, feeling the satisfying exhaustion that came from a weekend spent in creative flow. She'd written more in the past two days than she had in the previous two years combined. The story that had been forming in her mind for years had finally found its voice, and she had found her confidence.

She'd attended the Single Mothers Support group on Friday night and had left Will with Daniel. Baby steps. When he'd asked to practice pitches on Saturday, she'd said yes and had turned to her screen to work on her story and distract herself from worrying about Will. It felt good to have some time for herself, and she also felt guilty for those feelings. She didn't want to be like her own parents. She never wanted Will to feel like a burden. He was her family—the only family she'd ever really had.

Adaline's attention returned to her computer, her gaze moving across her screen, re-reading the last sentence she'd written in Laiken's story. Was her story any good? Would anyone want to read it when she was finished?

A knock on her classroom door broke her stream of thoughts.

"Hi, Marcus." She gestured for her third-grade student to come inside her classroom. He often stopped by at the end of his day as he made his way back to homeroom from the small resource classroom where he worked on math. His general education teacher didn't mind because she knew Marcus didn't have the best support system at home. Any encouragement or attention he could get here with school staff was good for him. "Hey, would you like to hear a story before you go back to class?" she asked him.

Marcus struggled with reading and often became frustrated to the point of tears. But he had an active imagination and loved being read to, which made him the perfect test audience for her story.

"Is it a long story?" he asked, plopping down into the chair across from her.

"Well, I've only written the first few chapters," Adaline said, picking up a stack of printed papers. "But I thought you might like to hear about a boy named Laiken who has a disability. Then something happens and he discovers that he's braver and stronger than he ever imagined."

Marcus's eyes lit up. "Yeah. That sounds like a good one, Ms. Harper."

Grinning, Adaline began to read, watching his face carefully as she introduced the main character of her story, Laiken, a ten-year-old boy who used a walker and struggled to fit in with his classmates. She described Laiken's frustration with being different, his longing to be like the other kids and his mother's gentle guidance as she helped him see he was made exactly as he was meant to be.

As Adaline read about Laiken's first day on a baseball team, where a kind coach helped him discover his natural talent for strategy and encouragement of the other team members, Marcus leaned forward in his chair.

"What happens next?" Marcus asked when Adaline paused. "Does Laiken get to play in the big game? Does he make friends with the other kids?"

Adaline's heart swelled with the validation she hadn't known she needed. "Well, I haven't written that part yet."

"You have to finish it!" Marcus exclaimed. "I need to know how it ends. Will you write more so you can read it to me during our next lesson?"

Adaline laughed, amazed by how invested he'd become in just a few pages. "I'll do my best. In fact, your excitement makes me want to go home tonight and write the next chapter right away."

"Yay!" he cheered.

The bell rang, signaling the end of the school day, and Marcus reluctantly gathered his things. "Don't forget to write more!" he called over his shoulder as he headed back to his classroom.

A few minutes later, Will entered her room. "Mom, why are you in such a good mood? You look like you just got a present. Or a huge compliment."

She kind of did. Before she could answer, Will's expression shifted. "Are you thinking about Coach Daniel?"

The question caught her off guard. Had her feelings become so obvious that even her nine-year-old son could read them? "Actually, I was just reading the story I've been writing to one of my students," she said, gesturing to the stack of paper. "He really seemed to enjoy it."

Will's grin could have powered the entire school. "The story about me?"

"It's not exactly about you," she clarified, "but you definitely inspired the main character. His name is Laiken, and like you, he has a disability that makes him feel different from other kids. But he discovers that God made him special for a reason."

"Did Coach Daniel inspire the dad in your story?"

Adaline looked down at her notebook, mentally reviewing

the character she'd created—the father figure who appeared in chapter three to help Laiken navigate his challenges. Dark hair, hazel eyes, a life on a farm, a role as a Little League baseball coach who saw potential where others saw limitations.

She hadn't even realized how much she'd been inspired by Daniel, but it was true. Daniel was the perfect father figure, and any boy would be blessed to have him in a parenting role, including Will.

"Mom?" Will's voice was concerned now. "Did I say something wrong?"

Adaline shook her head quickly. "No, sweetheart. You're right. Coach Daniel may have inspired that character a little bit." She cleared her throat and changed the subject quickly. "Are you excited about this weekend's baseball game?"

Will practically launched himself off the ground, holding tight to his walker for balance. "Yes! Coach Daniel says if we win, we're one step closer to making the championship!"

Adaline laughed at his enthusiasm. As she watched his joy, she promised herself that she would tell Will the truth soon. The excitement he felt about having Coach Daniel as his coach would be nothing compared to learning that Daniel was actually his father. Christopher had been amazing to him for the two short years that he was in Will's life, but it wasn't fair to continue to lie to Will or anyone for that matter. It wasn't fair to herself either. If people turned their backs on her after she confessed, then she'd deal with that.

"You know what, Mom?" Will said, settling back down and studying her thoughtfully. "The mom in your story is definitely modeled after you."

"Oh, I don't think so, sweetheart. The mother in the story is… Well, she's the kind of woman I would love to be. She's strong and wise, and she always knows the right thing to say."

"That's exactly like you," Will said with such sincerity that she couldn't help but believe him. "You always know how to make me feel better when I'm sad. You always help me see that being different isn't bad, it's just...different. And you taught me that verse about how God knit me together in my mother's womb. 'I am fearfully and wonderfully made,'" he announced.

Adaline's throat tightened. "Yes, you are. Will?" she said softly. "What if I told you that sometimes moms make mistakes? That sometimes they keep secrets because they're scared, even when keeping secrets isn't the right thing to do?"

Will considered her question. "You always forgive me, so I guess I'd forgive you too. Plus, that's what God says we have to do, right?"

Adaline's eyes filled with tears. Will had never held a grudge in his young life. He forgave quickly and loved unconditionally, seeing the best in everyone around him. Maybe that was proof that she was a better mother than she realized.

"I love you so much," she said, pulling him into a hug. "More than you'll ever know."

"I love you too, Mom. And I can't wait to read the rest of your story."

She couldn't wait either to finish writing and to see what God had in store for her and Will's real-life story. She hoped it included Daniel. And that it would have a happy ending.

Daniel adjusted his Prairie Dogs cap and surveyed the baseball diamond as the visiting team warmed up on Saturday. The afternoon sun cast long shadows across the field, and the stands were filling with parents clutching coffee cups and team spirit signs.

This was Will's first competitive game, and Daniel was so proud of him. Not just because Will was his son, but because of Will's perseverance and determination.

As the Prairie Dogs took their positions for warm-ups, Daniel noticed two players from the opposing team, the Millerville Hawks, standing near their dugout. They were pointing in Will's direction and laughing, their young voices carrying across the field.

"Look at that kid with the walker," one of them said, loud enough for Daniel to hear. "How's he supposed to play baseball? This is going to be an easy win."

Daniel's hands clenched into fists at his sides. The protective instinct that roared to life in his chest was unlike anything he'd ever experienced. Suddenly, he understood with perfect clarity the challenges that Will faced every single day and the cruelty that children could inflict without even understanding its impact.

He remembered being that age himself, making thoughtless comments about kids who were different. It was never out of meanness, but out of ignorance. But knowing that didn't make hearing it directed at his son any easier to bear.

When the game started, Daniel made a decision that felt right in the moment. He kept Will in the dugout during the first few innings, telling himself he was saving Will from embarrassment or injury.

"Coach Daniel?" Will asked eventually. His voice was small and disappointed. "Am I not playing today?"

"Yeah, of course you're playing, buddy. I was just waiting for the right moment."

Daniel noted Will's slumped shoulders and downcast gaze. Will didn't want to be left out. He'd been left out all his life. The way to protect him wasn't by keeping him on the bench; it was by equipping him with the skills and encouragement to do everything he wanted.

In the bottom of the fifth inning, with the score tied 3–3, Daniel called Will's name. "You're up to bat, son."

The word slipped out before Daniel could stop it, but Will

didn't seem to notice. Daniel helped Will to the plate with his specialized lightweight bat, the one they'd practiced with for hours during their private coaching sessions.

As Will took his stance, Daniel became acutely aware of the whispers and pointing from the stand, not from children this time, but from adults who should have known better. Parents leaning toward each other, some shaking their heads, others looking skeptical about Will's ability to contribute to the game.

Daniel's eyes found Adaline in the bleachers and he noted the worried expression on her face. How many times had she sat in those stands, or at the school, watching her son face this kind of scrutiny? How many times had she felt this helpless anger at people who couldn't see past Will's disability to the remarkable child underneath?

"Coach Daniel?" Will looked up at him with serious eyes. "Want to know a secret?"

Daniel crouched down beside him. "What's that, buddy?"

"The secret to success," Will said, "is ignoring the meanies. They're just jealous because they can't be as brave as me."

Daniel was speechless. Here was his nine-year-old son, facing down judgment and cruelty with a wisdom that many adults never achieved. Will wasn't just well-adjusted despite his challenges; he was thriving because of how he'd learned to meet them.

And Daniel had Adaline to thank for that. Whatever mistakes she'd made, whatever secrets she'd kept, she had raised their son to be confident, resilient and kind. She had taught him to see his differences as strengths rather than limitations.

"You're absolutely right." Daniel patted his shoulder. "Now show them what you can do."

Stepping up to the tee, Will took his stance the way Daniel had taught him during their practice sessions. He pulled back his lightweight bat and connected it with the ball with a solid crack that sent the ball sailing toward the gap between center and right field.

The crowd erupted in cheers as Brian, Will's designated peer runner, took off toward first base. The system they'd constructed allowed Will to fully participate while acknowledging the realities of his disability.

As Brian rounded second base and headed for third, Daniel realized this was going to be more than just a hit; it was going to be a home run. Without thinking, he scooped Will up from where he'd hit the ball, lifting the boy onto his shoulders. Then he veered left toward home plate as Will's peer runner reached the same spot. Will's delighted laughter mixed with the roar of the crowd.

"Home run!" the umpire called as Brian crossed the plate, and the Prairie Dogs' dugout exploded in loud cheers.

Daniel set Will down near home plate, watching his son beam with joy as his teammates surrounded him with high-fives and congratulations. The game wasn't over just yet. They still had one more inning, but at this rate it looked like the Prairie Dogs might be having ice cream tonight. The winning kind.

"That home run with that kid with the walker shouldn't have counted," a man called out from the bleachers, his voice loud enough to carry across the field. "They basically cheated by giving out free points just because the kid has a disability."

Daniel took a step toward the man, ready to come to his son's defense. Then Will's words echoed in his mind. *The secret to success is ignoring the meanies.*

Taking a deep breath, Daniel forced himself to turn away and focus on his team, not the small-minded comments of people who didn't understand the challenges Will faced.

# *Chapter Seventeen*

Adaline's heart was still pounding from the excitement of Will's home run as she approached Daniel, wiping sweat from his brow with a towel, his hair damp and his cheeks flushed from the excitement of the game. Will had wanted to ride together for the first game, just like they had for the initial practices. The more time Will spent with Daniel, the more he wanted, and honestly, she felt the same way.

"Daniel," she said as he approached, gaining his attention. "Hi. That was a great game."

He nodded. "I'm just the coach."

"You're more than Will's coach," she said quietly. And Adaline knew Daniel was ready to fully step into the role that she'd denied him for so many years.

"I want to be more," Daniel replied. "I'd like to talk, Addie. I want to discuss some things."

Adaline's stomach clenched. She suspected that Daniel was ready to tell Will the truth about their biological relationship and develop a formal co-parenting plan. Maybe he'd even hired a lawyer and was planning to take Will away from her altogether.

Looking at Daniel's face, and seeing the softness there, she didn't think that was true though.

"There's a lot I want to tell you, Addie."

"I want to tell you things too," she said quickly.

Before Daniel could respond, Will barreled toward them,

nearly tipping over his walker. "Why don't we go get ice cream? That way we can celebrate my home run!"

Adaline started to reject the idea. How could they have the conversation they needed with Will listening to every word?

"I think that's a great idea, Will," Daniel said, surprising Adaline. "It's a baseball tradition that if you hit a home run, you get ice cream afterward. Two scoops with sprinkles."

Adaline tilted her head. "I thought the tradition was ice cream if you lost a game."

Daniel reached out and ruffled Will's hair. "The tradition is ice cream if you do your best, regardless of the score."

Adaline grinned at Daniel and felt that familiar squeeze on her heart. She knew they couldn't discuss what they needed to with Will around, but there was something comforting about Daniel wanting to spend time with her without immediately diving into the heavy conversations. It almost felt like he wanted to be her friend, possibly even more, despite her betrayal.

As they walked toward the parking lot, Will grabbed Daniel's hand with his free one, practically bouncing with excitement despite his walker. "Coach Daniel, did you know my mom is writing a book? And you're one of the characters in it!"

Daniel raised his eyebrows at Adaline.

"Will, that's not exactly what I—"

"There's this boy in the story who's a lot like me, and he has a dad who's just like you. He lives on a farm and coaches baseball and has dark hair and your color of eyes and everything."

Adaline wanted to disappear. She tried to correct Will and explain that the character wasn't specifically based on Daniel, but Will wasn't finished.

"And my mom is a character too. She's the mommy, and the daddy in the story is just like Coach Daniel!"

"Will," Adaline said weakly.

"Mom always says that God has a plan for everything,"

Will told Daniel, looking between the two adults with satisfaction. "Maybe God's plan is for you two to get married so I can have another dad."

The innocent faith in Will's voice made it hard to be upset with him.

"Will, we can talk about this later, okay?" Adaline didn't want to ruin his excitement from the game. She also wasn't sure what Daniel was thinking. When she looked over, he seemed to like the idea. Was she imagining that? Was that what Daniel wanted too?

An hour later, after ice cream and carefully neutral conversation about baseball and school, Will had fallen asleep in the back seat of Daniel's truck, his face peaceful and his new baseball mitt still clutched in his small hands. Despite the fact that they'd taken both vehicles to the ice cream shop, Daniel insisted on driving Will home rather than waking him.

"I can carry him inside myself," Adaline said as they pulled into her driveway. "I've been doing it for years."

Daniel turned off the engine and looked at her seriously. "You've done enough parenting on your own to this point, Adaline. It's time you allowed someone else to lend a hand. It's time Will had a father."

The words hung between them. Daniel lifted Will easily from the back seat, cradling the sleeping boy against his chest as if he'd been doing it his whole life. Adaline led them through the house to Will's room, watching as Daniel gently laid their son in his bed and pulled the covers up to his chin.

After she'd kissed Will good night and turned off his light, Adaline found Daniel waiting for her in the living room, his hands clasped behind his back as he studied the family photos on her mantelpiece.

"I can leave if you're not comfortable having this conversation so late at night in your home," he offered quietly.

Adaline shook her head and settled onto the couch, her heart pounding. "No. I'm ready to discuss moving forward. I want to discuss everything."

As Daniel sat down across from her, Adaline felt a peace wash over her. The walls were down and all she felt was trust and admiration for the man in front of her. The father of her son. Their son together.

Daniel settled onto the couch across from Adaline, the space between them charged with the weight of everything they needed to say. The house was quiet except for the soft tick of the grandfather clock in the hallway.

"I want you to know that I'm still hurt," Daniel began. "I won't pretend that learning about Will after all these years wasn't difficult for me. I'm thrilled, of course. I feel like I have a lot of lost time to make up for, but I want to do what's best for Will. Even if that means waiting longer to tell him the truth. I just need to know our plan moving forward. I need to know there's an end in sight and a day coming when Will can call me Dad instead of Coach."

Adaline clasped her hands tightly in her lap. "I want that too, Daniel. I want you to be more than just a coach and a friend to Will. Both of you deserve that."

"I do have reservations," Daniel continued. "What if Will isn't happy to have me step into the shoes of his late father?"

Adaline shook her head. "He will be. He loved Christopher, but he only has the memories captured in his baby album."

"I'm also worried that he might be upset with you," Daniel said. "And I don't want that, Addie. I know you're an amazing mother. The evidence shows in just how determined and kind and loving Will is. I don't want any of this to damage his relationship with you."

Adaline looked up at him with surprise. "You're concerned about protecting me from Will's disappointment?"

Daniel shrugged. "Of course I am."

"Daniel, I would deserve Will's anger," she said softly. "But Will has never been a boy to get upset easily. He's always been quick to forgive. It's one of his greatest gifts. He has the heart of Christ when it comes to grace."

Daniel reached across the space between them and gently took her hand in his. "Addie, I need you to know something," he said, looking directly into her eyes. "I've been praying nonstop since I discovered that Will is my son. And God has given me peace about this situation."

He watched tears gather in her eyes as his words sank in.

"Some part of me even understands why you did what you did, Addie," he said. "You were young and scared, and you were facing what I'm sure felt like an impossible situation. I care about you, Addie. Of course I do. I never stopped caring."

He stopped himself before he said anything more revealing like the fact that he'd also never stopped loving her. Deep down, all he wanted was to be a family with her and Will and to build the life they might have had if circumstances had been different. He wasn't sure if Adaline felt the same way, though.

Adaline gently pulled her hand from his to swipe a tear from under her eye. Daniel instantly missed the warmth of her hand in his.

"Will is going to be thrilled to learn that you're his father, but I know he'll also be confused. What kid wouldn't be?" Adaline rolled her lips together, seeming to hesitate on telling him what she was thinking. "You've seen how Will's imagination works. He's already developed fantasies about us falling in love and getting married." She laughed quietly. "I just… I just don't want to give him false hope about being a family. In the traditional sense."

Daniel understood her caution even if it frustrated him. He sensed that Adaline was going to ask for more time, and if that's what she thought was best, he'd agree. "You're right. We need to be careful about how we handle this."

Adaline cleared her throat and offered a definitive nod. "We should tell him tomorrow," she said. "After church."

Daniel felt his jaw drop. "Tomorrow?"

"Yes. I think that's best. After church, Will and I will go to your parents' house for lunch. I've already accepted your mom's invitation. After we eat, we can sit down, together, and explain everything to Will."

"Are you sure?" Daniel asked, excitement and sudden panic filling his body. He watched Adaline nod, assessing her body language to make sure this was what she wanted. He didn't want to pressure her. They needed to be on the same page about Will from this point on. "Okay. Well, I should probably tell my parents first then. They deserve to know before Will does."

Adaline bit her lower lip, giving him pause. "Actually, your mother already knows."

Daniel straightened, creating distance from Adaline and trying to process what she'd said. If his mother knew she had a grandchild, nothing would have stopped her from spoiling him or her rotten. Will's farm-themed birthday party flashed through his mind along with her perfect attendance to every baseball practice. Daniel had thought she was watching him coach, but now he realized his mom had been watching her grandson. "You told her?"

"She figured it out."

Daniel chuckled despite everything. "I never was able to hide anything from my mother. Apparently, you can't either."

They both smiled.

"We can't keep this under wraps much longer," she said.

"Not in a small town like Prairie," Daniel agreed.

"It's long past time to tell the truth. I've been running from what God was asking me to do for months," Adaline admitted. "He's been working on my heart to tell you the truth for a long time. I kept making excuses, finding reasons to wait, but He never stopped pressing me to do the right thing."

"God's been working on me too," Daniel said quietly. "Teaching me about forgiveness and urging me to step into His calling on my life. It seems we're both pretty stubborn when it comes to listening to Him."

"I'm listening now," Adaline said softly.

The grandfather clock chimed, signaling a new hour.

"God is telling me something right now too," Daniel said, rising to his feet. If he stayed much longer, they might end up talking all night. What would Will think if he woke up to Coach Daniel at the breakfast table?

Adaline lifted her eyebrows. "Oh? What is He saying?"

Daniel gestured toward the front door. "That it's late and the respectable thing to do is say good night."

He started walking and was almost to the door when her hand caught his, stopping him in his tracks.

"Daniel?"

He turned to face her, noting how beautiful she looked in the living room's dim lighting, her hair pulled back in a messy bun and her eyes bright. "Yes?"

"Thank you. For forgiving me. For giving me a second chance that I don't deserve."

Daniel glanced down at their interlocked hands, swallowing hard against the emotion tightening his throat. "If we're going by God's standards, none of us deserve anything. It's only by Christ's sacrifice and God's grace." He returned his gaze to hers. "If we're going by my standards, Addie, you deserve everything." Including his heart.

# *Chapter Eighteen*

The familiar comfort of Prairie Community Church's sanctuary felt different this Sunday morning as Adaline sat in the wooden pew beside Will, watching Pastor Matthews take his place behind the pulpit for the first time since his illness. His color had returned, and there was strength in his voice as he opened his Bible and began to speak about God's faithfulness during trials and the joy that comes in the morning after weeping through the night.

"Psalm 30:5 reminds us that 'weeping may endure for a night, but joy cometh in the morning,'" Pastor Matthews declared, his voice carrying the authority of someone who had walked through darkness and emerged into light. "Sometimes God allows us to go through difficult seasons not to punish us, but to prepare us for the blessings He has waiting on the other side."

Adaline felt the words resonate in her chest, thinking about her own long night of secrets and shame that was finally giving way to the possibility of redemption. Joy.

When the service ended, Will could hardly contain his excitement about going to the Matthewses' home for lunch. "Mom, can I ride with Coach Daniel and Pastor and Mrs. Matthews? Please? I want to tell them about my home run and show Pastor Matthews my new baseball mitt!"

Adaline glanced at Daniel, who nodded his agreement.

"That sounds like a wonderful idea, sweetheart," she said, though her heart clenched slightly at the thought of watching her son drive away with his father and grandparents, family he didn't even know were his yet.

She watched as Daniel helped Will into the truck, noting the booster seat he'd purchased to keep in his vehicle. One more clue that this was real and Daniel wasn't going anywhere. Daniel made sure Will's seat belt was properly fastened before climbing in the back passenger seat of the cab. Mrs. Matthews settled into the front next to Pastor Matthews, who was seated at the wheel. For a moment, Adaline felt like an outsider looking in. She quickly pushed those negative thoughts aside. The Matthews family loved her, and she loved them. Nothing was going to change, not for the worse at least.

As she followed their truck through the familiar streets of Prairie, Adaline gripped the steering wheel and prayed.

"God, You know my heart. Your Word says for us not to be afraid, but I am," she whispered aloud. "Will is a good boy and I've never known him to get mad at anyone, but what if today's revelation changes things between us? What if he feels like I betrayed him? I certainly lied to him. I'm his mother," she prayed, telling God everything on her heart.

In her spirit, that still, small voice silenced her. She felt God remind her that she was His child. In the same way that Adaline loved and protected Will, God would do the same for her. Fear not.

Peace washed over her, filling every space in her body, leaving no room for anxiety.

"Thank You, God. Thank You for providing Will with the most wonderful man I could have ever imagined. Daniel has shown himself to be mature and caring, patient and kind. And he already loves Will so much. I can see it in everything he does."

Tears of gratitude spilled off her cheeks. "Thank You that Will is going to have wonderful grandparents who already adore him. Thank You that his life is about to become so much brighter and richer. And thank You that my life is brighter too." She was writing again. She had a sense of family now. It wasn't just her and Will against the world anymore. It never was.

Adaline pulled into the Matthewses' driveway and sat in her car for a moment, watching as Daniel helped Will out of the truck while Pastor and Mrs. Matthews headed toward the house. When Daniel was done, he turned in her direction and headed toward her car.

"We can do this," he said, offering her his hand. "Together."

Adaline slipped her hand in his. Then she stepped out of the car and looked up at him, marveling at how safe she felt in his presence. When he reached up to wipe a tear from her cheek, her heart fluttered with something that went beyond a co-parenting partnership. At least that's what she wanted from Daniel.

"I read the chapter from the book you're writing last night," Daniel said, his voice filled with warmth and admiration. "I hope you don't mind. You left the folder in my truck after I dropped you and Will off."

Adaline's eyes widened. "You read it?"

Daniel grimaced. "I'm sorry. I was just trying to see what it was and then, well, I read one line and couldn't stop. Addie, it's great. I know I shouldn't have read it."

She'd considered letting someone read her work, maybe Beth, just to see if it was any good. "It's okay," she said. "You liked it? It's just the draft. I plan to polish it after I'm finished."

"It's incredible. You have real talent," Daniel continued, his tone sincere. "The way you've written about Laiken's journey so far, about finding purpose and belonging despite challenges…it's going to help so many children and their parents understand kids with disabilities."

He paused, a teasing smile playing at the corners of his mouth. "I especially liked the characters of the mommy and daddy. I think they're pretty great parents if I do say so."

Adaline released a nervous laugh. "They make a good team," she agreed.

"Like us," Daniel said, still holding her hand. He gave it a gentle squeeze.

As they walked toward the house together, Adaline breathed in the aroma of home-cooked food that drifted from the kitchen. It smelled like pot roast and fresh bread. She also thought she caught a whiff of Mrs. Matthews's famous apple pie. The aroma was reminiscent of family. A smell that felt like coming home.

She helped Mrs. Matthews serve the meal, falling easily into the rhythm of a family gathering, and when they all sat down at the dining room table, Pastor Matthews offered to say grace.

"Heavenly Father, we thank You for this food and for the hands that prepared it. We thank You for my health, and for allowing me to preach Your word again this morning. I praise You for giving me the privilege of doing what I love to do. We thank You for having our son home with us, and for having Adaline and Will as our guests. Bless this meal and our time together. In Jesus's name, Amen."

As they began to eat, Pastor Matthews addressed the group. "I would like everyone at this table to know that I spoke to Daniel a couple weeks back and I gave him an out if he wanted it. Now that I'm back on my feet and feeling better, I told Daniel that I could handle the farm and church responsibilities myself. I gave him my full support in heading back to Atlanta."

Mrs. Matthews nodded and smiled, implying she knew about this past conversation. Adaline didn't though. Daniel hadn't mentioned it to her. Somehow, though, the news didn't worry her. All of Daniel's recent words and actions told her that he was happy being back in Prairie. Any business dreams he'd once had were gone, replaced with a newly realized passion in serving his father's church and the community.

Daniel cleared his throat and met her gaze before scanning the other faces at the dinner table. "And I told Dad that I didn't want to leave Prairie. I've decided..." He looked around the table. "Well, I've decided to stay." He winked at Will and grinned. "A wise friend told me that the secret to success is to ignore the meanies and do what makes you happy."

Pastor Matthews laughed, recognizing that Will was likely that wise friend. "And what exactly makes you happy, son?" he asked Daniel.

Without hesitation, Daniel replied, "Spending time with my family."

The word *family* hung in the air like a promise.

"I've decided to pursue my original plan," Daniel continued. "I'm going to attend seminary classes part-time online and part-time in person. I'm excited about serving in the youth ministry. And—" he shrugged "—I guess I'll make money doing whatever work I can find until I'm ordained."

Mrs. Matthews reached over and patted her son's hand. "We still need help on the farm, you know."

Will piped up enthusiastically. "And I still need a coach!"

Everyone laughed, the sound filling the dining room with joy and the promise of a future filled with shared meals and celebrations.

"Well, then," Pastor Matthews said after a few minutes of

comfortable conversation, his voice strained with emotion. "I guess it's official. My son is home to stay, and I couldn't be happier. Or more blessed."

The afternoon sun cast long shadows across the pasture as Daniel watched Will carefully hold an apple out to Star, the gentlest of his father's horses. The mare took the treat delicately from Will's small hand, her nose tickling his palm and making him giggle.

"She likes me," Will announced as he reached for another apple from the bucket Adaline held.

"Of course, she does," Daniel said. "Animals can always tell when someone has a good heart."

They'd been out in the pasture for nearly an hour as Will fed the horses and listened to Daniel explain each animal's personality and quirks. But underneath his calm composure, Daniel felt his nerves building with each passing moment. Soon, they would have to return to the house. Soon, it would be time to tell Will the truth that would change all their lives forever.

Daniel caught Adaline's eye across the fence, and she gave him a small nod, silently agreeing that the moment had come. His heart began to race as fear crept in around the edges of his resolve.

Yes, Daniel was his coach, but what else did he have to offer? He had no money, no career prospects beyond his tentative plans for seminary. He was thirty years old and living with his parents, starting over from scratch. What kind of father figure was that for a boy like Will?

*Lord,* Daniel prayed silently, *give me the words. Help me be the father Will needs and not the failure I sometimes feel like.*

Almost immediately, a familiar peace washed over him,

the same peace he'd felt when he'd made the decision to stay in Prairie and pursue ministry. God's plans were not his plans, and God's timing was perfect even when Daniel couldn't see the bigger picture.

"Coach Daniel?" Will's voice interrupted his internal struggle. The boy had stopped feeding the horses and was looking up at Daniel with concern, his small hand reaching for Daniel's larger one. "Are you okay? You look like you're thinking really hard about something important."

Daniel's heart squeezed. He had so much love for this child. His child. Kneeling to Will's level, he looked him directly in the eyes, hazel like his. "Will, do you remember how scared you were to start playing baseball because you didn't know all the rules of the game?" Daniel asked gently.

Will nodded. "I was scared, but I was more excited than scared. I really wanted to learn."

Daniel marveled at his son's positive outlook. "That's exactly how I feel right now."

Will's brow furrowed. "But Coach Daniel, you know everything about baseball. You taught me everything I know."

Both Daniel and Adaline laughed at Will's earnest assessment.

"I'm not talking about baseball this time, buddy," Daniel said. "I'm talking about something I don't know much about at all. I don't know a lot about being a father."

Will's confusion deepened, and Daniel could see the wheels turning in his young mind. "Are you going to be a dad, Coach Daniel?"

Adaline moved closer and knelt beside Daniel, facing their son with a mixture of love and apprehension in her eyes. "Will, sweetheart, Daniel already is a father."

"Will," Daniel said, his voice shaking, "this might not make sense at first, but we'll talk about it, as much as you need." He looked at Adaline for help as he struggled to find the words. "Will…"

"Will," Adaline took Will's hands in hers. "I want to talk to you about your father."

Will's brows bunched. "What about him?" he asked.

"The man you've always known to be your father loved you so much, Will. But that man wasn't your birth father." How did she explain what that even meant to a child of Will's age? "When God places a baby in their mother's belly, He uses bits and pieces of both the mom and the dad."

"Like a collage," Will said.

"Right." Adaline nodded. "Your collage is the very best parts of me." She looked at Daniel and pulled in a breath. "And the very best parts of Daniel."

Will's brows were bunched again. "What about my dad who died?"

"Oh, Will, he loved you as much as any father ever could." She ran a hand down his hair. "But he wasn't your birth father."

"I am," Daniel said, hesitancy in his voice.

Will's eyes widened. "Really?" His voice was filled with wonder rather than anger or betrayal. "I have the best parts of you in my collage too?" he finally asked, visibly assessing Daniel for their similarities.

"Afraid so. Is that okay with you, Will?"

Will grinned momentarily. Then his smile slowly faded as the wheels in his mind seemed to spin. "If you're my birth dad, why haven't you lived with us? Is it because of my disability? Is it because you didn't want me?"

The questions broke Daniel's heart. "No. No, that's not it at all. I just didn't know about you." He didn't want to cast any blame on Adaline or raise more questions in this moment. "I'm proud to have you as a son, Will. Any man would be blessed to have you in their family."

"So what you're telling me is that I am extra blessed because I have two dads instead of one?" Will asked, his smile returning in full force.

Daniel didn't mind sharing the title with another man who'd been willing to step up and love his son when he couldn't. "Can this dad have a hug?"

Will melted into his arms and Daniel fought against the tears forming in his eyes. He understood why it'd been so difficult for Adaline to release Will because now that Will was in his arms, Daniel never wanted to let go.

When Will finally pulled out of the embrace, he looked between his parents with the kind of joy that only children can experience when their deepest wishes come true. "Does this mean you two are going to get married like in the movies?"

Daniel's heart skipped as he looked at Adaline. "Well, buddy, some dreams are worth working toward."

"Are you talking about going back to seminary school?" Will asked, remembering their conversation at lunch.

"Yes." Daniel nodded. "That's one dream I'm working toward. But I have another dream in my heart now. A dream about a new beginning with you and your mom."

Adaline reached for Daniel's hand, her touch as warm as her smile. "I have that same dream," she said softly.

Will clapped his hands together. "Yay! It's just like in Mom's story. Coach Daniel is the dad and Mom is the mom, and now that you've found each other again, we're going to be a family forever."

Tears pricked Daniel's eyes. "One thing at a time, Will. All in God's time," he added.

As they sat there in the pasture, the sun warming their skin, Daniel marveled at how God had taken his and Adaline's mistakes and woven them into something beautiful. Ten years ago, he would never have imagined this moment, holding his son while the woman he'd never stopped loving smiled at them both with tears of joy in her eyes.

"I love you… Dad," Will said, testing out the new word. He looked unsure but as the word tumbled off his lips, he laughed softly and said it again. "Dad. I like the sound of that."

He liked the sound of that too. "I love you too, son," Daniel replied, and for the first time in his life, he felt like he was exactly where he needed to be, on the path to the future God had laid out for him. He reached for Adaline's hand and leaned over to whisper something for her ears only. "I love you, Addie. I always have and I always will. That's a promise." He held up his pinkie finger.

She pressed a soft kiss against his cheek, making Will giggle as he watched. "I love you too, Daniel Matthews," she said, curling her little finger around his. "A forever promise."

# *Epilogue*

The evening air was filled with the sounds of celebration as Daniel's family gathered on the back porch of the farmhouse. Just three months ago, they had feared Pastor Matthews might not see another birthday, but God had been gracious and granted him not only a full recovery but renewed strength for the ministry he loved.

Daniel watched his father laugh at one of Will's animated stories about school, amazed at how much had changed since his father's illness. Pastor Matthews was only preaching part-time now, sharing pulpit duties with Pastor Jason, though Jason had recently announced that God was calling his family to a new ministry opportunity in another state. While it was hard to say goodbye, the transition felt natural, like pieces of a divine puzzle falling into place.

Three years of intensive study in seminary school while working part-time at the church and farm wouldn't be easy but it'd be satisfying in a way that business school never had been for Daniel. Every morning when he opened his textbooks, he felt a confirming peace that let him know this was where God wanted him. It was where he was always meant to be.

Better late than never.

"Daniel, can I speak with you for a moment?" His mother's voice interrupted his thoughts. She gestured toward the kitchen, and Daniel followed her inside, leaving the sounds of celebration behind.

His mother moved to a cabinet above the sink and withdrew a small black velvet box, placing it in Daniel's palm. Instantly he knew what he was holding. Opening the lid, he took in his grandmother's diamond, nestled in a cluster of tiny rubies. It was a simple but elegant ring that had witnessed decades of faithful love.

"I can't wait to give it to her." Daniel studied the ring that had adorned his grandmother's hand for fifty-three years of marriage.

His mother nodded approvingly, her eyes bright with unshed tears. "I'd say you've waited long enough. Why wait any longer?"

Daniel closed the box's lid gently, his thumb tracing its worn edges. "I don't want to upstage Dad's birthday celebration. This is his day."

His mother cupped her hands along Daniel's cheeks, looking at him with the same loving expression she'd worn when he was five years old and afraid of the dark. The same warmness she'd offered when he'd been grieving his friend Carlos and when he'd rebelled against everything she'd ever taught him. A mother's love was unconditional. So was a father's.

"A parent only wants the best for their child, Daniel. Nothing would make your father more joyful today than to know that you, Adaline and Will are committing to a future together." Her voice grew softer, cracking with emotion. "You're home. Not just physically, but in heart and spirit. It's what we've been praying for all these years."

Daniel tucked the box into his jeans pocket. The weight of it felt like a promise. "We'll see," he told his mom. He wanted the timing to be perfect and he didn't want to propose until he felt that it was the right moment.

Returning to the backyard, Daniel found Will helping to clear dessert plates from the picnic table. "Hey buddy, can I talk to you for a minute?"

Will looked up with curiosity, pushing his walker to follow Daniel to a quiet corner of the porch. "What's up, Dad?" He giggled every time he said the word, the newness of it still exciting.

Daniel understood. The word still sent a thrill through his chest every time he heard it too. Dad. "Will, I want to ask your mom a question, but I need to talk to you before I do."

Will tilted his head. "Why me? What's the question?" His eyes rounded as he realized what it might be. "Are you going to ask my mom to marry you?" he practically yelled.

Daniel glanced around nervously, hoping Adaline wasn't around to hear.

"She's inside," Will said. "Is that it?" he asked again.

Daniel nodded. "That's it. I want to ask her to marry me. But first, I wanted to make sure I have your blessing."

Will's expression was answer enough. "Are you serious? That's what I've been praying every night for."

Daniel grinned back at his son, seeing himself in his eyes. He also saw Adaline, the woman he loved. "Well, if you're okay with it, then there's only one person left to ask."

Will practically bounced on his toes. "I've been waiting for this since the day I found out you were my dad! When are you going to do it?"

Daniel patted Will's shoulder. "Soon. How about we keep this a secret for now, okay? I want to surprise her."

Will mimed zipping his mouth shut. "My lips are sealed."

As the party began to wind down and guests started to leave, Daniel caught Adaline's hand. "Would you like to take a walk with me? Maybe check on the horses?"

She squeezed his hand but then looked for Will.

"He's with my mom," Daniel told her. "Just us. Is that okay?"

"It's perfect," she said, following him along the familiar path behind his family home.

It had become one of their favorite places to talk and dream together when they were teens and it felt the same now, years later.

They walked in comfortable silence for a moment as Daniel worked up the courage to pop the question.

"Will's physical therapist is so happy with how well he is doing," Adaline said, interrupting his thoughts. "She says he's made incredible progress preparing for baseball season. And did I tell you I heard from the publisher today?" Adaline talked quickly and excitedly.

"A publisher? What did they say?"

Adaline paused, her eyes dancing in the setting sunlight. "They want to publish my book!" Her voice was thick with emotion. "And they want me to write more books featuring children with disabilities. They said there's such a need for stories that help typical children understand and interact with kids who are different from them."

"I am so proud of you, Adaline. That's incredible. You're going to help so many families."

"I never thought this would be possible," she said, still holding his hand. "A year ago, I was just a single mother trying to get through each day. Now I have this amazing opportunity to make a difference, and Will has you as his father, and we have this beautiful life together..."

"About that..." Daniel's heart raced as he reached into his pocket, his fingertips brushing against the soft velvet. "There's something I want to ask you."

The sun was setting behind them, painting the sky in shades of pink and gold as Daniel dropped to one knee in the soft grass. For a moment, her brows furrowed, confusion sweeping through her features. Then her hands flew to her mouth as he slowly revealed the black box and pulled back the lid. "Our life is nearly perfect. There's just one thing that's not quite right."

Adaline blinked back tears. Was this a dream? She'd imagined this very moment so many times, but now Daniel was kneeling in the grass before her, holding out a diamond that caught the light brilliantly.

Once upon a time, she'd been a young teenage girl who knew beyond a shadow of a doubt that Daniel was the man she would marry. Ten years had passed though, and just when she'd thought she'd never find love, here he was proposing.

Daniel. The boy who had stolen her heart in high school detention. The young man who had broken it when he left for college. And now the godly man who had returned to redeem himself and keep the promise he'd made when they were young.

"Adaline," Daniel began, his voice steady despite the emotion threatening to overwhelm him, "ten years ago, I made the biggest mistake of my life when I left you. I thought I was doing the right thing, but I was really just letting my own fear and pride keep me from the life I was meant to have. God has brought us back together in His perfect timing, and I don't want to waste another day without you knowing how much I love you."

Tears pooled in her eyes as she sniffled and tried to gather her thoughts. She had cried so many tears over the man kneeling before her, never expecting him to return to her life, never imagining that God could transform their broken pieces into something so beautiful. The scared eighteen-year-old girl who had made desperate choices was gone, replaced by a woman who had learned to trust God's faithfulness even in the darkest seasons.

"I want to walk beside you as you pursue your dreams," Daniel continued. "I want to parent Will together and maybe add to our family someday. I want to serve God together and I want to build a life based on His love and grace. Addie, would you do me the greatest honor of my life and marry me?"

"Yes," she answered without a moment's pause. "I would love to be your partner in this life. I would be honored to be your wife."

As Daniel slipped his grandmother's ring onto her finger, Adaline thought of all the verses about God's perfect timing that had sustained her through the lonely years. Ecclesiastes 3:1 came to mind. *To every thing there is a season, and a time to every purpose under the heaven.* This was their season. A season of love, family and dreams that they could chase together.

Adaline threw her arms around Daniel's neck as he stood, and their kiss tasted of tears and laughter. When they finally pulled apart, cheers rang out from the direction of the house, where Will and Daniel's parents had apparently been spying on them from the porch.

"I love you," Adaline whispered against Daniel's cheek. "I never stopped loving you, not even when I thought I'd lost you forever."

"You'll never lose me again," Daniel promised. "We're going to write our story together from now on. A story of redemption and second chances and God's incredible faithfulness."

"I like the sound of that."

As they walked back toward the house hand in hand, Adaline marveled at the journey that had brought them to this moment. She hadn't grown up with a loving family or gone to church in her youth. Daniel and his parents had taught her what family looked like and what it looked like to serve God. And God was changing her relationship with her own father, which she'd never thought would happen. With God, though, anything was possible.

This was the life she'd never known she wanted and she was so thankful that Will would grow up with a family like the Matthewses.

"There's so much to celebrate," Mrs. Matthews said, welcoming them both with open arms as they reached the porch. "Welcome to the family, sweetheart," she whispered into Adaline's neck. "Although I've always considered you like a daughter."

Adaline shared a look with Daniel. *Thank You, Lord*, she silently prayed, full of gratitude and love. So much love. The kind that lasts forever.

* * * * *

Dear Reader,

Years ago, while sitting in my own local church, the seed for *Hometown Home Run* was planted in my mind while listening to my pastor talk about his own calling to ministry. He was a pastor's son and he also tried running from his calling, just like Daniel in this story. That's the extent of the parallel between the two tales. From there, my imagination took over, creating a story for the prodigal pastor's son of *Hometown Home Run* who, like so many in the Bible, tried to deny God's direction for them.

When Adam and Eve disobeyed God's instructions, they got evicted from the garden. When Jonah tried to escape God's request, he was swallowed by a whale! It isn't easy to walk the path that God puts before us, but in my experience, it's far harder if we run from it. When I was writing Daniel and Adaline's story, I wanted to create two characters who had made their fair share of mistakes—big mistakes!—because I wanted to show that we're all sinners and we all fall short of the glory of God. Surrendering our sins, however, allows God to transform what the enemy meant for destruction into a powerful testimony (if we allow Him to).

I hope you enjoyed reading *Hometown Home Run* as much as I enjoyed writing it!

Blessings,
*Annie Rains*